**'Do you forgi**

She didn't. It was

'I'm working on it,' she said, and he smiled. A gentle, rueful smile that coaxed a reluctant answering smile from her.

A smile that slowly faded when his eyes continued to hold hers and she saw the guilt in them replaced by something altogether darker, hotter, more disturbing. *Get out of here, Maddie,* she told herself as she felt her pulse kick up and every nerve-ending she possessed spring into life. *Get out of here, fast.*

'I…I ought to get back to my work,' she said, trying to jerk her eyes away from his, only to find she couldn't.

'Must you?' he said, and she swallowed, hard.

Oh, Lord, it would be so easy to like this man. Hell, she was halfway there already. But this time it wouldn't just be her who would get hurt if it all went wrong.

**Maggie Kingsley** says she can't remember a time when she didn't want to be a writer, but she put her dream on hold and decided to 'be sensible' and become a teacher instead. Five years at the chalkface was enough to convince her she wasn't cut out for it, and she 'escaped' to work for a major charity. Unfortunately—or fortunately!—a back injury ended her career, and when she and her family moved to a remote cottage in the north of Scotland it was her family who nagged her into attempting to make her dream a reality. Combining a love of romantic fiction with a knowledge of medicine gleaned from the many professionals in her family, Maggie says she can't now imagine ever being able to have so much fun legally doing anything else!

**Recent titles by the same author:**

THE SURGEON'S MARRIAGE DEMAND
DOCTOR AND SON*
THE SURGEON'S MARRIAGE*
THE PLAYBOY CONSULTANT*

**The Baby Doctors*

# THE GOOD FATHER

BY

MAGGIE KINGSLEY

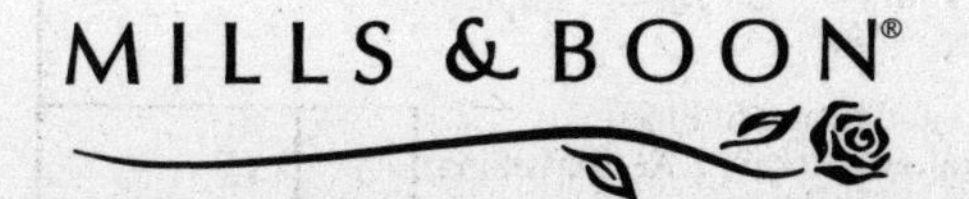

For Pat,
who has listened to my moans and groans over the past year without ever once telling me to shut up, and who has the most tolerant husband in the world in Peter



First published in Great Britain 2006
Harlequin Mills & Boon Limited,
Eton House, 18-24 Paradise Road, Richmond, Surrey TW9 1SR



ISBN 0 263 84733 0

Set in Times Roman 10¼ on 12 pt.
03-0506-54908

Printed and bound in Spain
by Litografia Rosés, S.A., Barcelona

# CHAPTER ONE

SOME days it just didn't pay to get up, Maddie decided as she sat in the office of the neonatal intensive care unit of the Belfield Infirmary, feeling her confidence evaporate with every passing second. Some days it would have been better if she'd simply pulled the duvet back over her head and forgotten all about trying to get a job, and today was undoubtedly turning out to be one of those days.

'It'll be a breeze,' her cousin Nell had said when she'd told her she'd got an interview. 'A little typing, some filing, answering the phone… You can do that, Maddie, no sweat.'

Dr Washington didn't seem to think so. In fact, judging by the way the specialist registrar's frown had deepened as he'd read through her application form, she'd be better off just leaving now and putting them both out of their misery.

'Miss Bryce,' he said at last, putting down her application form and sitting back in his seat, his brown eyes puzzled. 'Can I ask why you've applied for this job?'

*Because Charlie and Susie like to eat. Because my cousin Nell thought the job would be perfect for me but now I think she needs her head examined.*

'Well, I've always enjoyed working with people,' she said, all perkily upbeat and trying very hard to look as though a six-month contract to cover the maternity leave of the Belfield's

NICU secretary was the job she'd been secretly dreaming of since she'd been in kindergarten. 'The position sounded interesting—challenging—and I have secretarial certificates—'

'One in typing and one in computer studies, both gained at night school.' Dr Washington nodded. 'But, Miss Bryce, you're also a fully qualified nursing sister. A sister who was the ward manager in charge of the nursing staff of the neonatal intensive care unit of the Hillhead General for four years. So why in the world is somebody with your qualifications and experience applying for a secretarial post?'

On days like this she asked herself the same question. On really bad days, when she was trying to work out how she was going to be able to afford new shoes for Susie and new trousers for Charlie, she found herself wondering if this was all there was, if this was how it was always going to be, but she also knew that she didn't—and never would—regret her decision.

'I gave up nursing because I have children to look after,' she said. 'The hours a nurse has to work—the constantly changing shifts—it's not a viable option for me.'

'We have crèche facilities at the Belfield Infirmary.'

'Charlie is eight and Susie is fourteen. They're much too old for a crèche.'

The specialist registrar glanced down at her application form, then up at her again. 'Your daughter is *fourteen*? But…' He coloured slightly. 'It says here on your application form that you're twenty-nine.'

'The children aren't mine. My sister…' Maddie's throat closed as it always did when she had to talk about Amy. 'My sister and her husband John were killed in a car crash two years ago. John's parents…' *We'd like to help, Maddie, we really would, but we're much too old to look after children, and with Charlie the way he is…* 'They couldn't look after Charlie and Susie, and my parents are dead, so…'

'I see,' Dr Washington said gently. 'It can't have been easy for you—I'm sure it isn't easy now—but I'm afraid my neonatologist, Mr Dalgleish, expects the very highest standards from his staff, and though you have secretarial qualifications you don't actually have any experience, do you?'

'I gained a highly commended in my computer studies, and a merit in my typing,' she said, trying and failing to keep the desperation from her voice. 'I'm a fast learner. I work well under pressure—'

'Miss Bryce, I'm not disputing your enthusiasm or your willingness to work hard,' the specialist registrar interrupted awkwardly. 'In fact, I'm sure if Mr Dalgleish had been here to interview you and not been called away on an emergency he would have said the same, but we've had some very highly skilled and experienced secretaries applying for this post.'

She knew they had. She'd sat amongst them in the waiting room. Eight highly professional women all stylishly dressed in smart office suits while she, the last to be interviewed, had been all too horribly aware that she neither looked the part nor felt it.

'Dr Washington—'

'Mr Dalgleish will, of course, give your application his fullest consideration, and you should be notified in about a week if you've been successful.'

*But don't hold your breath.*

The specialist registrar didn't say the words—he didn't need to. This was the third interview she'd been to in as many weeks and she couldn't even get a job to cover somebody's maternity leave. Well, there'd be other jobs, she told herself. Maybe they wouldn't be as perfect as this one—close to home, and with her cousin Nell working as a sister in the neonatal intensive care unit it could almost have been like old times—but there'd be other jobs. There had to be. After not working for two years her savings were all but gone, and what little Amy had left her was almost gone now, too.

With an effort she pasted a smile to her lips. 'Thank you for your time, Dr Washington. I appreciate it.'

'It was my pleasure. I just wish—' She didn't find out what he wished because the door of the office suddenly opened and the specialist registrar got to his feet, an expression of clear relief on his face. 'Mr Dalgleish. I was just talking about you.'

'Saying something nice, I hope, Jonah,' a deep male voice replied, and as Maddie turned in her seat to face the newcomer her first thought was, *Nell, you lied.*

'He's tall and dark,' her cousin had said when she'd asked her what Gabriel Dalgleish was like. 'Around thirty-six, I'd say, and quite good-looking in a chiselled, square-jawed sort of way. Not bad to work for. An OK sort of a neonatologist, really.'

Well, he was tall, Maddie conceded as the neonatologist walked towards her. Six feet two inches tall, she guessed, and broad-shouldered with it. He was also dark. Thick black hair, piercing grey eyes and, as Nell had said, quite good-looking. But an OK sort of neonatologist?

Nope. No way. Her cousin knew as well as she did that there were only two types of neonatologist. There were the neonatologists who supported their staff, worked with them, encouraged them, and then there were the others. The men—and it was nearly always men—who ran their departments as their own personal fiefdoms, men who radiated power and arrogance from the top of their immaculately groomed hair to the tips of their highly polished shoes. One glance at Gabriel Dalgleish was enough to tell her this man was Genghis Khan and Attila the Hun rolled into one.

*Nell, you've got a lot of explaining to do.*

'Mr Dalgleish, this is Miss Bryce,' Dr Washington declared. 'She's one of the applicants for our post of departmental secretary.'

'Given the time of day, and the fact I was planning on interviewing the candidates myself, I'd gathered that much,' Mr

Dalgleish murmured dryly, failing entirely to say hello to Maddie, and she felt her hackles rise another notch. So the neonatologist used sarcasm as a weapon, did he? Well, she hadn't liked it when she'd been a nurse and she didn't like it now.

'Goodbye, Dr Washington,' she said, bestowing the warmest of smiles on him and giving Gabriel Dalgleish the coldest of cold shoulders. 'It was very nice meeting you.'

'Just a minute,' Gabriel Dalgleish said sharply as she began to walk towards the office door. 'Why haven't you applied to my department for a job as a nurse?'

'Why hasn't anybody ever taught you some manners?'

The words were out of her mouth before she could stop them and she saw a flash of anger appear on Gabriel Dalgleish's dark face, but she didn't care. She hadn't got the job, was never going to see this man again, so she could say whatever she damn well liked.

For a second there was complete silence in the office, then to her surprise a faint wash of colour appeared on Gabriel Dalgleish's cheeks.

'I apologise if my question seemed...a little brusque,' he said with difficulty, 'but I would appreciate an answer.'

Dr Washington was glancing from her to his boss in open-mouthed fascination, and for a second Maddie hesitated, but she supposed the neonatologist had apologised so the least she could do was meet him halfway.

'As I've already explained to Dr Washington,' she said evenly, 'I have two children to look after. And before you suggest a crèche,' she added, 'my children are too old for one and a childminder is out of the question.'

'That's your only reason?'

His grey eyes were fixed on her, searching, intent. What was he getting at—what was he trying to find out? She hadn't the faintest idea and neither, it appeared, did Dr Washington.

'Gabriel, I think Miss Bryce has already explained—'

'Let her answer, Jonah.'

Part of her—a very large part—longed to tell him she wouldn't have wanted to work as a nurse in his department even if he could have arranged for her to be paid double the national nursing wage with a free car thrown in for good measure, but she'd already been quite rude enough.

'Yes, that's the only reason,' she said, and for a fleeting moment an odd look appeared in Gabriel Dalgleish's grey eyes. A look that almost seemed like triumph. But before she could say anything he'd turned away and begun sifting through the application forms on his specialist registrar's desk.

Was that all he wanted to say? It looked as though it was, but she glanced questioningly across at Dr Washington to discover he looked as bemused as she felt.

'Is there anything else you'd like to ask Miss Bryce?' he said uncertainly, and Gabriel Dalgleish didn't even turn round.

'No, but I'd like her to wait outside for a few minutes,' he replied.

*And would it be too much of an effort for you to tell me so yourself, you big jerk?*

Of course it would. He was the head honcho, the top banana. He didn't speak directly to minions—and why the hell should she wait outside? She hadn't got the job, couldn't understand now why he'd even asked her to come in for an interview when he must have seen from her application form that she was totally unsuitable—but if he wanted her to wait, she'd wait. It wasn't as though she had anything else to do, and with a brief smile at Dr Washington, she headed for the waiting room.

'That has to be a record even for you, Gabriel,' Jonah observed as soon as the door of his office was safely closed. 'Managing to be very rude to a complete stranger in the space of two minutes.'

'I'd say Miss Bryce is no slouch herself in the rudeness stakes,' the neonatologist said dryly, and Jonah grinned.

'What happened with the emergency call in Maternity?'

'The baby died.'

Gabriel's closed face didn't invite further questioning and Jonah knew better than to probe. Instead he picked up the scattered application forms on his desk and put them in his in-tray.

'For the record,' he observed, 'the next time you find yourself suddenly unavailable to interview candidates I'd appreciate it if you could reschedule. Eight women, all bar one with identical qualifications and experience….' He grimaced. 'Nightmare. The only way I could narrow them down was by ruling out those who seemed a bit officious, those who had irritating laughs, those—'

'Cut to the chase, Jonah. Who would you pick?'

'Ruth Haddon. She didn't laugh like a hyena, didn't make me feel five years old, has sixteen years' secretarial experience—'

'I want Miss Bryce.'

The specialist registrar blinked. 'You want…? Gabriel, she's the least qualified of all the applicants, has absolutely no experience—'

'And in four months Lynne Howard will be emigrating with her family to New Zealand and I'll need a skilled NICU sister to replace her as ward manager. Madison Bryce is perfect.'

Jonah opened his mouth, closed it again, and when he finally spoke it was slowly and carefully.

'Gabriel, I hate to break this to you but Miss Bryce didn't apply for Lynne's job, she applied for Fiona's. She doesn't want to be a nurse. She has kids—'

'I don't care if she has a zoo,' the neonatologist interrupted. 'The minute I saw her application form I was on the phone to the Hillhead General, and the references they gave her were quite outstanding.'

'Gabriel, you're not *listening* to me,' Jonah protested. 'Madison Bryce doesn't *want* to return to nursing. Her kids—they're not ordinary kids. They're her niece and nephew and she's looking after them because their parents died in a car crash two years ago.'

'Kids are kids,' Gabriel replied dismissively. 'Once we get her into the department, let her see what she's been missing, I guarantee she'll jump at the chance of stepping into Lynne's shoes after she's gone to New Zealand.'

'You honestly think a woman who refuses to have her children looked after by a childminder is suddenly going to change her mind simply because she's worked here as a medical *secretary*?' Jonah exclaimed, and Gabriel threw him a look of exasperation.

'Of course she will. Nobody in their right mind would willingly throw their career down the toilet on the strength of some ridiculous antipathy towards childminders and it's up to us to make her see she's making a big mistake.'

Jonah stared at him silently for a second, then shook his head. 'You don't have children, do you, Gabriel?'

'You know I don't,' the neonatologist retorted. 'I'm not married, and neither are you, so what's your point?'

'No point. Just an observation.'

'Then it's a stupid one. Look, trust me on this one, Jonah,' Gabriel continued as his specialist registrar opened his mouth to argue. 'If we can keep Miss Bryce sweet for four months, we'll have Lynne's replacement in the bag.'

A small smile curved Jonah's lips. 'You're going to keep the woman who told you that you had no manners sweet for four months? This I have to see.'

'Jonah…'

'OK—OK.' The specialist registrar held up his hands in resignation. 'You're the boss and if you want Madison Bryce, then Madison Bryce it is. Reading between the lines, I'd say she needs the job.'

*She also looks as though she needs one,* Gabriel thought with a sudden and quite unexpected qualm. How old did her application form say she was? Twenty-nine. He would have said she was older. Of course, those dark shadows under her too-large brown eyes didn't help. Neither did the extreme whiteness of her skin, which contrasted so sharply with the riot of short curly auburn hair which framed her cheeks and forehead, but she didn't simply look older than her twenty-nine years, she also looked tired. Tired, and harassed, and stressed.

'I just hope my replacement doesn't expect a social life or too many hours' sleep,' Fiona had said at her leaving bash, 'because she sure as shooting won't get either in this department.'

But that was just Fiona's pregnancy hormones talking, he told himself. All women became irrational and emotional when they were pregnant.

But what if it hadn't been just her hormones talking? Fiona was a highly experienced medical secretary and if she'd found the workload tough, how much more difficult was it going to be for a woman with no experience, a woman who already looked exhausted and stressed?

'Gabriel…?'

Jonah's eyes were fixed on him curiously and Gabriel let out a huff of impatience. Hell's bells, it wasn't as though secretarial work was rocket science, and as for Madison Bryce looking stressed…he would have looked stressed, too, if he'd been throwing his career away on the strength of a quite irrational prejudice. Giving her the job would make her see that her future lay in nursing and, if it also solved the question of how he was going to replace Lynne Howard in four months, it wasn't being selfish. It was a purely practical and sensible solution for everyone.

'Let's go and tell Miss Bryce the good news,' he said.

'You want me?' Maddie said faintly, completely convinced she must have misheard. 'You're offering *me* the job?'

'If you want it,' Gabriel Dalgleish replied.

Did she? This morning she had. This morning she'd thought

it the answer to her prayers but that had been before she'd met him. Two minutes in his company had been more than enough to tell her he was cold, arrogant and supercilious, and she'd spent too many years as a nurse working for obnoxious neonatologists to want to repeat the experience.

*Oh, for heaven's sake, Maddie. Nobody's expecting you to bond with the guy. He'll be your boss, you'll be the NICU secretary, and even if he's the boss from hell the contract will only last for six months and at the end of it you'll not only have some money in the bank, you'll also have something to put in those big blank spaces on application forms marked 'Experience'.*

'Yes, I want the job,' she said quickly. 'When do you want me to start?'

'Next Monday.'

*Monday?* She'd have to ask the school whether it would be all right for Charlie and Susie to arrive there half an hour earlier every day, and she'd have to enroll them in some after-school activities because she wouldn't finish work until five. Susie would sulk and Charlie… Unconsciously she shook her head. She'd figure out how she was going to deal with Charlie later.

'Monday will be fine,' she said.

'Why don't I take you along to the unit, show you around?' Gabriel suggested, heading out of the waiting room and down the corridor towards the door marked NEONATAL INTENSIVE CARE UNIT. 'Not that there's anything you won't be familiar with. Though the Belfield Infirmary was built in Victorian times, we've managed to attract quite substantial funding over the past three years and can now offer three levels of care. Intensive Care for the most seriously ill babies, Special Care for those who need some tube-feeding, oxygen support or light therapy, and—'

'Transitional Care to prepare the babies for going home,' she finished for him, then bit her lip. 'Sorry. Force of habit.'

'Not a problem,' the neonatologist murmured, shooting a

glance at Jonah, which she didn't understand. 'In fact...' He paused as his pager began to beep and, when he unhooked it from his belt, he let out a muttered oath. 'Jonah, can you start the tour and I'll catch up with you later?'

He was gone in an instant, and Jonah smiled ruefully at her. 'It looks like you're stuck with me again, Miss Bryce.'

'I think I can stand that.' She chuckled. 'And, please, call me Maddie.'

'Only if you call me Jonah. And, please, no jokes about whales, sinking ships or bringers of bad luck,' he added. 'Believe me, I've heard them all.'

'You think a girl christened Madison is in any position to take cheap shots at your name?' Maddie protested, and the specialist registrar laughed as he began tapping a series of numbers into the keypad on the neonatal unit door.

'We change the security code once a month,' he explained. 'Fiona used to think up the combination based on birthdays and anniversaries so I guess it's your job now. It's a sad indictment of our society that we need a security system, but...'

What was even sadder—pathetic, really—was the overwhelming feeling of nostalgia she experienced when the door of the unit swung open. It had been two years since she'd worked in an NICU and yet it could have been yesterday. The smell of antiseptic, the overpowering heat because premature babies lost heat more quickly than full-term ones, even the cork board covered with baby photographs left by grateful parents—everything was so familiar.

'Lynne, this is our new secretary, Maddie Bryce,' Jonah declared, breaking into her reverie when a small, middle-aged nurse appeared. 'Maddie, this is Lynne Howard, our ward manager, and the best nursing sister in the Belfield.'

'Flattery will get you everywhere, Jonah.' The sister laughed. 'Good to have you on board, Maddie.'

'Everything OK this afternoon?' the specialist registrar asked.

'Nice and quiet apart from Baby Ralston. We've just finished his obs and as Gabriel has ruled out the bradycardia being caused by a heart defect I'd say we're looking at possible apnoea.'

'I'll set up a pneumogram and—'

'You'd like a coffee.'

'I'm getting predictable.' Jonah sighed, and the sister grinned.

'Nah, you're just a caffeine addict. Maddie, would you like a coffee?'

'If it's not too much trouble.'

'No trouble at all, and sorry about the medical jargon,' Lynne continued as Jonah disappeared through the door marked SPECIAL CARE. 'Bradycardia—'

'Is an abnormal slowing of the heart rate, and apnoea is when a baby simply "forgets" to breathe. I used to be a nurse,' Maddie added as the sister's eyebrows rose. 'An NICU sister to be exact, but I have children to look after, so…'

Lynne nodded sympathetically. 'It's the hours, isn't it? Never knowing for certain what days you'll be working—even what shifts. I'm actually leaving the unit myself soon,' she continued, ushering Maddie through to her small office and switching on the kettle. 'My husband has been offered a job in New Zealand so in four months time it's goodbye Glasgow and hello to the land of the long white cloud.'

'You must be really excited,' Maddie observed, and the sister sighed as she spooned coffee into two mugs.

'Part of me thinks, wow, what a great opportunity for my husband, our kids, but the other part… It's going to be a real wrench leaving my friends, a job I love, but…' She shrugged. 'I guess family always comes first.'

*Always*, Maddie thought.

'Sorry about the mess,' Lynne continued, moving a pile of files from a chair so Maddie could sit down, 'but I'm a nurse short this afternoon. Sister Sutherland had a family problem.'

Maddie's cheeks reddened. 'I'm afraid I'm the problem. Nell's my cousin,' she explained as Lynne stared at her, confused. 'I needed somebody to look after the kids when they came home from school and Nell knew I couldn't get a sitter…'

'Then you're *the* Maddie. The one Nell's always talking about—Charlie and Susie's aunt?'

Maddie nodded and to her surprise Lynne's face lit up with delight.

'Nell is going to be so pleased you got the job. She's been stressing for days about you going for an interview, but she wouldn't tell us where the interview was. Do you want to phone her—give her the good news? There's a phone downstairs in the communal staff room that we can use for personal calls.'

'Thanks, but I'd rather tell her when I get home.' *When I can also ask her what the hell she thought she was doing, telling me Gabriel Dalgleish was an OK sort of a neonatologist.*

Which brought her to something she very much wanted to ask Lynne, but asking a ward manager whether her boss had been born a complete dickhead or whether he'd just worked hard to become one didn't seem like a wise move.

'How long has Mr Dalgleish been head of the department?' she said instead, after Lynne had made the coffee.

'Almost three years.'

'He seems… ' Maddie paused to choose her words carefully. 'Very focused.'

The sister stirred her coffee for a second. 'His aim is to make our department not just the best in Glasgow, but the best in Scotland.'

'Ambitious,' Maddie observed, stirring her own coffee equally deliberately. 'What's he like as a surgeon?'

'I've lost count of the number of preemies he's pulled back from the brink when the rest of us had given up hope, and to watch him operate is an education.'

'That good, huh?'

'What Gabriel doesn't know about preemies could be written on a postage stamp.' Lynne put down her spoon and met Maddie's gaze. 'He is also, without exception, the biggest, coldest, out-and-out bastard it's ever been my misfortune to work for.'

'Thought so,' Maddie said, and the ward manager chuckled.

'He's wonderful with the babies but when it comes to interacting with people... It's like there's something missing. He just can't—or won't—see that people have feelings, needs, even homes they might occasionally want to go to. And don't ever disagree with him. If you do—'

'I'm mincemeat?'

'Got it in one.'

'Sounds like I'm in for a fun six months,' Maddie said ruefully, and Lynne grinned.

'Welcome to Alcatraz.'

The unit felt like a prison, too, when Gabriel eventually joined them. One minute Jonah, Lynne and the neonatal nurses were laughing and joking, and the next... Iceberg time, and the ridiculous thing was that Maddie knew it didn't have to be like that. A happy atmosphere didn't necessarily mean a slack ward, but convincing Gabriel Dalgleish of that? She'd have more success convincing Nell that she'd never be thin no matter how many crazy diets she tried.

A scowl creased Maddie's forehead. Which reminded her. She had a bone to pick with her cousin. A big one.

'Maddie, I knew you were looking for work, and if I'd told you he was the boss from hell you would never have applied for the job,' Nell protested, gazing longingly at the contents of the cookie jar for a second before helping herself to an apple instead. 'Some people like him.'

'Name one.'

'OK, all right, nobody likes him,' her cousin admitted, then smiled as the kitchen door opened. 'Hey, kids, your clever auntie's got herself a job.'

'Does that mean I can have the trainers I want—the ones with the light-up soles?' Susie demanded, dropping her schoolbag beside the freezer.

Maddie did some quick mental calculation. 'Yes, you can have the trainers. Cheese quiche and salad in half an hour, so you've time to start your homework.'

'Homework's boring,' Susie muttered, but she picked up her schoolbag and trailed back out of the kitchen instead of arguing, which had to be a first.

'How was school, Charlie?' Maddie asked.

'OK.'

He stood beside the kitchen table, a solemn undersized little boy with large blue eyes and pale blond hair, and she knew his day had been anything but OK, but there was no point in pushing him for information.

'You've got a job,' he said, scuffing his foot across the vinyl floor.

'Nothing is going to change, Charlie,' she said gently. 'You'll just have to go into school a little earlier, and stay on for the after-school activities until I get home from work. Apart from that, you're not even going to know I've got a job.'

'I liked knowing you were here during the day,' he muttered, and Maddie's heart clenched. Lord, but there were times when he looked so much like Amy it hurt.

'Charlie—'

'I have homework to do.'

He'd gone before she could stop him and she let out an uneven breath. At least he'd talked about her job. OK, so he was obviously unhappy about it, but at least he'd talked. There'd been times during the past two years when he hadn't said anything for days. Awful days, heart-breaking days.

'He'll be OK, Maddie.'

Nell's eyes were on her and she managed a watery smile. 'I guess so, but will I?'

'Surrounded by all those gorgeous, available doctors at the Belfield?' Her cousin grinned. 'Course you will.'

Maddie shook her head as she slipped the cheese quiche into the oven. 'If they're gorgeous, they're not going to be interested in me.'

'Will you stop putting yourself down like that?' Nell said angrily. 'You have lovely eyes—stunning hair—'

'And I'm off men for the duration,' Maddie interrupted, knowing that the words *and you're beautiful* weren't coming because she wasn't.

'Maddie, just because Andrew was a dipwad does not mean you should give up on the entire male population,' Nell declared, throwing her apple core into the bin. 'There's loads of nice guys at the Belfield. There's Gideon Caldwell in Obs and Gynae—except he and Annie are very happily married—but there's David Hart in Infertility…' Nell frowned. 'Actually, he's happily married, too.'

'Nell—'

'Lawrence Summers in Men's Surgical is single, but he's so vain he'd eat himself if he was chocolate. Jonah is single—What?' Nell protested as Maddie started to laugh. 'What's so funny?'

'Gideon, Gabriel, David and Jonah. It sounds like some sort of Old Testament convention.'

'You didn't make any jokes about Jonah's name, did you?' Nell said quickly. 'Everyone does, and it's so unfair when he's such a nice guy. OK, so maybe he hasn't got that wow factor, but—'

'Does Brian know you're checking out other men's wow factor?' Maddie laughed, only to see her cousin's face set. 'Joke, Nell, *joke*. Though I still think Brian needs his head examined for letting you stay in Glasgow while he waltzes off to the US for a year, engagement ring on your finger or no engagement ring.'

'Brian wanted to get some experience of working as an anaesthetist in another country before we got married.'

*And it didn't occur to him that the two of you might go there together?*

'Nell—'

'Anyway, we're not talking about me,' Nell continued firmly, 'we're talking about you.'

'I've given up dating. I'm going to buy a cat or a dog. It's safer.'

'Maddie—'

'Are you staying for dinner?'

'I'd love to, but I promised Lynne I'd do the night shift in exchange for having this afternoon off.' Her cousin walked towards the kitchen door, then stopped. 'Gabriel Dalgleish is single.'

Maddie dropped the spoon she was holding. *'Are you out of your mind?'*

'Sixty per cent of all relationships start with couples meeting at work, and you're going to be in an office just two doors down from him. It's perfect, Maddie.'

'It's insane,' Maddie protested, bending down to retrieve the spoon. 'Even if I was looking for somebody—and I'm not—the man's an overbearing, arrogant jerk.'

'I bet you could loosen him up.'

'By doing what—putting whoopee cushions on his seat, exploding pens on his desk?' Maddie shook her head. 'Nell, get a grip.'

'I'm not asking you to marry the guy—'

'I'd have you certified if you did.'

'But you're good with people,' Nell continued, 'and if you could loosen him up, make him more approachable, you'd earn the undying gratitude of everyone at the Belfield.'

'I'm sure that would look really good on my tombstone. Can't I just buy him a hamster—bring out his caring side that way?'

'Maddie, you're not taking this seriously,' Nell protested, and Maddie laughed.

'Of course I'm not. Nell, you're my cousin, and I love you dearly, but do you honestly think Gabriel Dalgleish would be any better for me than Andrew was?'

Nell appeared to give the idea some thought, then her eyes twinkled. 'Well, he's a lot taller. OK, OK, it's a dumb idea,' she continued as Maddie waved her spoon threateningly at her, 'but I worry about you. You're only twenty-nine and you're letting your whole life slip by.'

'Nell, I *am* fine.'

And she *was* fine, Maddie thought after her cousin had left. OK, so maybe sometimes she was lonely, and sometimes it would have been nice to have somebody to cuddle, but Gabriel Dalgleish…

She let out a snort of laughter. Just being civil to him for the next six months was going to be tough enough, but to go out with him, to become involved with him? She'd rather sign herself up for root-canal treatment.

# CHAPTER TWO

GABRIEL gathered up the files on his desk, then sat back in his seat, his eyes red-rimmed with fatigue. 'I think that pretty well brings you up to date on everything that happened in the unit last night, Jonah, apart from the fact that while Baby Ralston seems to be finally remembering to breathe on his own, we'll still keep him on medication for another forty-eight hours.'

'Do you reckon that kid's parents are ever going to give him a first name?' Jonah said as he made a note on his clipboard.

'Yesterday they were considering Simon or Thomas. The day before it was Quentin or Robert. Looks like they're working their way through the alphabet.' Gabriel reached for his mug of coffee. 'Oh, and Tom Brooke from Obs and Gynae is coming down to the unit later.'

'The Scott baby?'

Gabriel nodded. 'It's a tricky situation because Mrs Scott isn't technically a Belfield obs and gynae patient after the argument she had with them last year, but I told Tom he could come.'

'I still don't know why Mrs Scott behaved as she did,' Jonah observed. 'Tom wasn't being unreasonable. He just wanted her to wait a year to see if the cornual anastomosis he'd performed to unblock her Fallopian tube was a success, and he said if she wasn't pregnant by the end of a year, he would start her on IVF treatment.'

'Her argument was that, at thirty-six, her time was running out.'

'But a successful cornual anastomosis gives a woman a sixty per cent chance of conceiving naturally,' Jonah protested. 'Whereas the success rate for IVF is only around thirty to thirty-five per cent, not to mention being one of the most emotionally fraught treatments a woman can undergo.'

'I know that, you know that, both Obs and Gynae and the infertility department tried to tell Mrs Scott that, but she wouldn't listen,' Gabriel said, rubbing his eyes wearily. 'The person I blame is the head of the private infertility clinic she went to. He not only completely ignored her past medical history—but to implant four eggs into her when any reputable infertility expert knows you shouldn't implant more than three...'

'With the result that three of her babies were born stillborn last night, and the surviving baby weighs just 720 grams.' Jonah sighed. 'Not good.'

'No,' Gabriel murmured, and it wasn't. Although advances in modern technology meant that many babies now survived who would previously have died, there was a limit to how small the baby could be, and at 720 grams little Diana Scott was very small. Perhaps too small.

He finished his coffee in one gulp but, as he reached for the cafetière on his desk to pour himself another, Jonah gazed at him severely.

'That'll be your third in forty-five minutes.'

'Not that you're counting.'

'I'm counting,' Jonah said. 'Gabriel, you don't need more caffeine. You need sleep. You've been at the hospital for the past seventy-two hours and nothing's going to happen here that I can't cope with.'

'Even so—'

'Damn it, Gabriel, I'm your specialist registrar, not some

first-year medical student you can't trust!' Jonah snapped, and a half smile curved the neonatologist's lips.

'I agree, but you're also not my mother, nor do I ever envisage choosing curtains with you, so quit with the advice.'

'Gabriel—'

'OK, I'll make a deal with you. I'll go home after lunch.'

'But—'

'The first twenty-four hours are always the most critical for a preemie, and Diana's a full sixteen weeks premature.' Gabriel raked his fingers through his hair, making it look even more dishevelled than it already was. 'I have to be here.'

Jonah let out a huff of exasperation. 'Gabriel, you don't have to prove anything to anyone any more. Three years ago this department was underachieving big time but you've pulled it round, and not just pulled it round but made it the best in the city. You've *succeeded.*'

'Perhaps.'

'There's no 'perhaps' about it,' the specialist registrar exclaimed. 'Hell's bells, you were even right about Maddie Bryce. I know she's only been with us a week but she's efficient, on the ball—'

'When Tom arrives, I think I'll ask her to go along with him to the unit,' Gabriel said over him, and Jonah groaned.

'Don't you ever think about anything except work?'

A small smile curved the neonatologist's lips. 'Nope.'

'Then you should—especially in Maddie's case,' Jonah observed. 'All these errands you keep sending her on to the unit. She's not stupid, Gabriel, and if she finds out you're trying to manipulate her…'

*I'm dog meat,* Gabriel thought, remembering the anger he'd seen in her large brown eyes when she'd told him he had no manners.

'I think I know how to handle Miss Bryce,' he said, and Jonah grinned.

'So how come you're still calling her "Miss Bryce" when the rest of us are calling her Maddie? You always used to call Fiona by her first name.'

He had, but then, Fiona had been plump and jolly and non-threatening.

Not that Madison Bryce was threatening. She just made it abundantly clear that she didn't like him. Well, he could live with that. He'd always thought personal popularity a highly over-rated commodity and, though he might occasionally have liked to have seen her dark brown eyes smile up at him the way they smiled at everybody else, he wasn't going to lose any sleep over it if they never did.

'I like her,' Jonah continued. 'She's good company, easy to talk to—'

'So when's the wedding?' Gabriel interrupted with an edge to his voice. An edge that was all the more ridiculous because he wasn't interested in Madison Bryce, not in a personal way.

'I'm only saying she's nice,' Jonah protested. 'She has lovely hair, too.'

*Beautiful hair,* Gabriel thought. Hair that gleamed like fire when the late May sunshine streamed through her office window. The kind of hair which just cried out for a man to touch it, to see if it was as soft and as springy as it looked, but to be able to touch a woman's hair without having your teeth knocked down your throat you had to get to know her, and after Evelyn he'd decided to take a break from dating. A very long break.

'Maddie isn't going to change her mind about returning to nursing, you know,' Jonah continued, clearly misinterpreting his frown. 'I've been speaking to her about her niece and nephew and it's obvious she adores them.'

'She can adore them as much as she wants and still be an NICU nurse,' Gabriel declared irritably, and she could.

Good grief, it had been proven over and over again that children who were looked after by childminders performed just as well academically as children who were looked after by their mothers. He had himself. He'd hardly seen his mother when he'd been young and it hadn't done him any harm.

'Gabriel—'

'Any problems with the staff this morning?'

'The man with the one-track mind.' Jonah sighed, and Gabriel leant further back in his seat with a half-smile.

'Perhaps, but you still haven't answered my question.'

Jonah busied himself with his clipboard. 'Everything's fine. There was one very minor tiny incident, but I sorted it out.'

'What very minor tiny incident?' Gabriel said, his smile disappearing.

'It was no big deal, Gabriel,' Jonah said awkwardly. 'Student Nurse Barnes wasn't aware of the rule, and the soft toy was only in the incubator for a couple of minutes—'

Gabriel sat up so fast his feet hit the floor with a crash. 'What soft toy—which incubator?' he demanded, and with a sigh of resignation Jonah told him.

'Only a complete and utter idiot would have allowed a parent to put an unwrapped soft toy into an incubator with a preemie but then, *complete and utter idiot* just about sums you up, doesn't it, Nurse Barnes.'

*Oh, nice one, Gabriel,* Maddie thought, pausing in the middle of her work to listen to the sound of his footsteps growing fainter in the corridor outside, followed by the slamming of a door, which probably meant Nurse Barnes had disappeared into one of the toilets to have a good cry. *I bet that really makes Naomi think she made the right career choice.*

She glanced at her watch. Twelve o'clock. He was late this morning. Normally he'd managed to tear somebody apart by midmorning. He must be slipping.

'Maddie, have you managed to print out those case notes for

me yet?' Jonah asked, hurrying into her office, looking harassed and anxious. 'The ones I forgot had to be up to date by today?'

'Just finished.' She smiled, clicking the 'Save' button on her computer and slipping some paper into the printer. 'I've even made duplicates for you, and filed the originals.'

'Maddie, you're a lifesaver.'

'And Gabriel Dalgleish is an arrogant, overbearing sadist.'

Jonah sighed. 'You heard what he said to Nurse Barnes.'

'Jonah, the people out in the street probably heard what he said to Naomi Barnes!' she exclaimed. 'OK, so she should have known that all soft toys need to be wrapped in plastic before they're put into an incubator to guard against possible infection, but she's a student nurse, only in the unit to observe, and yelling at her—destroying all her self-confidence—isn't the best way to give her information.'

'He's had a bad morning—'

'I don't care if he's had a lifetime of major catastrophes,' she interrupted. 'Nothing gives him the right to talk to people the way he does.'

A tide of uncomfortable colour crept across the specialist registrar's cheeks. 'I know he can sometimes be a little rough—'

'*A little?*'

'But Gabriel and I have known one another since med school and he sets himself—and others—very high standards. There's no room for failure in his life. His background…let's just say his family has a lot to answer for, but he truly doesn't mean to be cruel. He just speaks before he thinks.'

'Oh, yeah, and I expect Captain Bligh's men were always saying, "Well, old William might be a tad over-enthusiastic with the cat o' nine tails but deep down he's all heart."'

Jonah shook his head and laughed. 'At least he's never ripped into you, has he?'

It was true, he hadn't, Maddie realised with a frown as the specialist registrar sped away. Not even on her first morning when she'd screwed up the office database by hitting 'Escape' on the computer instead of 'Enter'. He'd simply smiled tightly and said it could have happened to anyone. It was weird. It was more than weird. It was unnerving.

'Miss Bryce?'

*Talk of the devil.*

'Yes, Mr Dalgleish?' she said, quickly closing down Jonah's file before she could do something stupid, like deleting it.

'I'd like you to meet Dr Annie Caldwell from Obs and Gynae,' he replied, ushering forward the young woman who was standing behind him. 'Annie, this is Madison Bryce, our new departmental secretary.'

'Madison,' Annie Caldwell repeated. 'That's a most unusual first name.'

'I'm afraid my parents had a very quirky sense of humour,' Maddie said ruefully. 'They named me after the hotel I was conceived in. I suppose it could have been worse. I could have been conceived in the Pig and Whistle or the Dirty Duck.'

Annie Caldwell laughed, but not a glimmer of a smile appeared in Gabriel's grey eyes, and Maddie wondered if he ever laughed. Probably not. He probably considered laughter a waste of time and energy.

'My friends and family call me Maddie,' she continued.

'It suits you,' Annie said. 'Don't you think it suits her, Gabriel?'

Gabriel didn't look as though he cared one way or the other and it was on the tip of Maddie's tongue to say he didn't look like a Gabriel—a Lucifer, perhaps, but not a Gabriel. But she didn't.

'Would you like a cup of coffee, Dr Caldwell?' she said instead.

'I'd love one, and please call me Annie. Whenever anybody says "Dr Caldwell", I always think my husband has arrived and caught me doing something I shouldn't.'

Maddie laughed, but not so much as a muscle moved on Gabriel's dark, lean face. *Oh, for crying out loud.* Maybe she ought to buy those whoopee cushions or, better yet, one of those telescopes which left you with a big black ring around your eye when you looked through it. It would give his staff a laugh if nothing else.

'I don't want to hurry you, Annie,' Gabriel said, 'but I really think we should go to the unit now and have coffee later. Tom will be anxious for an update on Diana's condition, especially as he couldn't come down here himself as he'd planned.'

Annie nodded. She also didn't look as though a visit to the unit was high on her list of 'must do' activities and Maddie wondered if the young doctor didn't like neonatal units. A lot of medics didn't. They found the smallness of the babies, their all-too-obvious vulnerability, difficult to cope with. But before she could say anything Gabriel had begun steering Annie towards the door, only to pause as though something had just occurred to him.

'Miss Bryce, Lynne was asking for the blood-test results for the Thompson twins, so why don't you come along to the unit with us and give them to her?'

*Because I'll bet my first pay cheque Lynne won't want them,* Maddie thought angrily. Lynne never wanted anything he kept sending her along to the unit with, so why the hell did he keep on doing it?

Well, this would be the fastest visit to the unit she'd ever made, she decided as she grabbed the blood-test results from her out-tray and followed Annie and Gabriel with ill-concealed bad grace. A brief hello to Lynne and she'd sneak away and get on with the work she was supposed to be employed to do.

'Gabriel told me you used to be a ward manager in the NICU of the Hillhead General,' Annie observed, as Gabriel keyed the security code into the pad on the neonatal door, 'but you gave up nursing because you had to look after your niece and nephew.'

'*Wanted* to,' Maddie replied. 'Not *had* to.'

'Ah.' Annie smiled. 'Big difference.'

An ill-disguised snort from Gabriel showed what he thought of that opinion, and Maddie waited for him to voice what he was thinking, but he didn't.

'We think Diana may have PDA—patent ductus arteriosus,' he said instead, ushering them both into the unit and down the narrow corridor towards the intensive care ward before Maddie could escape into Lynne's office, as she'd planned. 'The ductus arteriosus is a blood vessel which allows blood to bypass a baby's lungs while it's in the womb. Normally it closes just before birth, but in some premature babies it can remain open, flooding the vessels in the lungs and causing respiratory problems.'

'Is it curable?' Annie asked, and Gabriel nodded.

'We'll perform an ultrasound scan to confirm she does have PDA, then we'll try medication to close it. If that doesn't work we'll operate.'

'Operate?' Annie repeated, when they drew level with Diana's incubator and she stared down at the little girl. 'But she's so tiny, Gabriel. That little hat she's wearing—it would barely cover a tennis ball. How can you operate on someone so tiny?'

'Smaller babies than this have survived major surgery,' he replied, pulling on a pair of surgical gloves and reaching into the incubator to ease Diana further up the heat-retaining cover she was lying on. 'Our current record for survival is a baby who weighed only 560 grams.'

'But look at her—all those tubes and wires,' Annie said, distress plain in her voice. 'She's even got a catheter in her little umbilical stump, and a pulse oximeter taped to her foot. She's so small, Gabriel, and to inflict all of this on her…'

'Annie, I wouldn't do it if it hurt her,' Gabriel said and, as he gently stroked the little girl's cheek, Maddie felt her throat tighten.

He cared. He really cared about this baby. One look at the expression in his eyes as he gazed down at Diana Scott was enough to tell her he would have crawled over broken glass if he thought it would help her. How could he feel and show such compassion towards this tiny scrap of humanity and yet be so appallingly insensitive to adults? It didn't make sense. *He* didn't make sense.

'Sorry to interrupt, Mr Dalgleish,' Nell said as she appeared at their side, 'but the radiology technician is here to take X-rays of Bobbie Duncan, and you said you wanted a word with him.'

He nodded. 'Sorry about this, Annie, but—'

'It's OK—I know how it is,' she replied, but when he'd gone she let out a shuddering sigh. 'I don't know how anybody can work here. I know you do wonderful work—tremendous work—but...'

Annie's face was white and strained and instinctively Maddie moved closer to her. She'd been right about the young doctor. She didn't like neonatal units, and she didn't like them big time.

'Babies are a lot tougher than they look, Annie,' she said softly. 'I know it can be upsetting to see them surrounded by a mass of tubes and wires but they don't stay like that. Once we've discovered what's wrong with them we can treat them and they start to put on weight, to develop, and when their parents eventually take them home... When that happens, then working in an NICU is the most wonderful job in the world.'

'But not all babies go home, do they? Some die.'

'Yes, some die,' Maddie admitted, 'but every year our techniques are improving, our medical equipment is improving, and more and more babies are surviving.'

Gently, tentatively, Annie put her hand against the side of Diana's incubator. 'But very premature babies—babies of only three or four months gestation—they can't ever survive, can they?'

Maddie shook her head. 'A foetus of that age doesn't have sufficient heart and lung development. Maybe some time in the future—when science is more advanced than it is now—somebody will be able to invent an incubator that can exactly replicate a woman's womb, but until then…'

'Those babies always die.'

There was pain and heartache in Annie's voice. A pain that Maddie sensed was due to something more than a simple dislike of neonatal units, but before she could say anything the young doctor had stepped swiftly back from the incubator.

'I have to go. My department must be wondering where I am, and you must be on your lunch hour.'

She was, but Maddie didn't care.

'Are you all right?' she said, and Annie nodded.

'Of course I am, so if you'll excuse me…'

She strode out of the ward, leaving Maddie gazing after her. She could see Nell mouthing, *What's wrong?* behind Gabriel's back, but she shook her head. She didn't know what was wrong, but something most certainly was.

'If you're off to lunch,' Lynne said as she passed her, 'the special in the canteen today is lasagne.'

Lasagne sounded good. Getting out of the unit before Gabriel dreamt up yet another errand to send her on sounded even better, and quickly she gave Lynne the Thompson twins' blood results and slipped away.

The canteen was crowded and noisy and exactly what she needed. So, too, was the lasagne, and she was just wondering how the cook could make such excellent pasta and yet such very lousy coffee when suddenly a grey-haired woman wearing a migraine-inducing sweater sat down at her table, and smiled at her with absolutely no sincerity at all.

'You're Madison Bryce, NICU's new secretary, aren't you?' she said, her eyes fixed on her speculatively. 'I'm Doris Turner, Obs and Gynae's secretary, although of course I always consider myself to be primarily Mr Caldwell's personal secretary.'

Maddie wondered if Annie's husband felt similarly blessed, but she knew it was important to make friends—or to be at the very least on speaking terms—with the staff at the hospital, so she managed a smile.

'Mr Caldwell's a lovely man—a really lovely man,' Doris continued. 'He was a widower for five years before he met Dr Hart, as she was then. Annie's a nice girl but...' Doris lowered her voice. 'She has a child by another man, you know. A little boy.'

'Mrs Turner, I really don't think you should be telling—'

'Poor Mr Caldwell,' Doris sighed, as though Maddie hadn't spoken. 'As if the tragedy of his first wife's death with ovarian cancer wasn't bad enough, he and Dr Hart were only married for four months when she had a miscarriage. Of course, I did think at the time that she shouldn't have carried on working while she was pregnant, and I know Mr Caldwell felt the same, but Dr Hart knew better, and now—almost a year on—she still hasn't managed to conceive again.'

So that was why Annie had become so upset in the neonatal unit. It must have brought it all back to her, the baby she had lost, the baby who could never have survived at such an early gestation. Tom Brooke should never have sent her down to the unit but, then, men never did think.

'I understand Mr Dalgleish is a terrible tartar to work for,' Doris continued.

'He certainly likes his department to be run efficiently,' Maddie said noncommittally, 'but, then, most neonatologists do.'

'I've heard it's a lot worse than that,' Doris said. 'I've heard he rules his department with a rod of iron. Do this, do that, jump when he says jump.'

'Then you heard wrong,' Maddie snapped. 'He's a very well-liked head of department.'

Doris gazed at her incredulously and Maddie couldn't blame her. Nobody in NICU liked Gabriel, so why in the world was she lying about him? She scarcely knew the man, and what she knew she didn't like, but all her instincts told her Doris Turner was trouble. The woman clearly fed on gossip, both from getting it and from passing it on, and she had no intention of providing her with any juicy titbits.

She glanced down at her watch and started with fake amazement. 'Good heavens, is that the time? I really must be getting back to the department—'

'We secretaries all have an hour for lunch,' Doris interrupted. 'In fact, I was wondering if you'd like to come along to my office. I could make you a proper cup of coffee instead of the disgusting dishwater they serve here, and we could talk more privately.'

'That's most kind of you, but—'

'I think it's important that we secretaries stick together, don't you?'

Maddie stared into Doris's speculative little eyes and knew that the last person in the Belfield she wanted to stick to was Doris. Desperately she looked round the canteen for an escape route, and suddenly saw one. It wasn't an escape route she would normally have chosen but desperate situations called for desperate measures.

'I'm so sorry, but I have to go.'

'Go?' Doris repeated. 'But—'

'My boss seems to want a word with me,' Maddie said, getting to her feet, 'so if you'll excuse me...'

'But—'

She could still hear Doris protesting as she darted across the canteen to where Gabriel was sitting, but she didn't care. Escaping from her was all that mattered and if she was jumping out of the frying pan and into the fire she'd worry about that later.

'Mr Dalgleish, do you mind if I join you?' she said breathlessly when she reached his table.

He looked startled, and she wasn't surprised. She would have been startled, too, if a panic-stricken woman had suddenly appeared without warning at her side.

'Of course I don't mind,' he said. 'What can I do for you?'

'Talk to me,' she said, sitting down quickly. 'It doesn't matter what you say just so long as you look as though whatever you're saying, and whatever I'm saying, is of earth-shattering importance.'

He gazed at her blankly for a second, then glanced across the canteen, and to her surprise a muscle quivered slightly in his cheek.

'Ah. The dreaded Doris.'

Maddie nodded with relief. 'So, if you could just talk to me, and try to look intent on what I'm saying, she won't try to join us.'

'Look intent?'

Good grief, did she need to spell it out for him?

'Just stare at me, OK?' she said. 'Just talk to me and stare at me as though I'm giving you the code numbers for a secret Swiss safety-deposit box.'

The muscle in his cheek quivered even more. 'A secret Swiss safety-deposit box. OK, I think I can do that.' He moved his empty lunch plate to one side, put his elbow on the table and leant his chin in his hand. 'How's this?' he murmured, staring so deeply into her eyes that she gulped.

Boy, but when he faked intent he really went for it. In fact, in this light, he looked a little like Susie's latest pin-up. Except, of course, that the actor in question had brown hair and green eyes, and a sort of come-hither twinkle in his eyes, whereas Gabriel Dalgleish had black hair and grey eyes which didn't twinkle at all, but…

'I thought this was supposed to be a two-sided conversation,' he muttered out of the corner of his mouth, and she blinked.

'Sorry?'

'I'm doing my best here in the intent and talking stakes, and you're sitting there looking like a rabbit caught in the headlights of a car. If you want to convince Doris that our conversation is really important and necessary, you're going to have to look considerably more animated.'

'Oh. Right. Animated.' She flushed slightly. 'Um...' *Pull yourself together, woman.* 'I'm sorry, but what were you talking about?'

He rolled his eyes heavenwards. 'You wouldn't make a very good undercover agent.'

'I've never needed to,' she replied, stung. 'But Doris—'

'KGB-trained.' He nodded as she tried to smother a laugh and failed. 'Leastways, that's what most of us reckon.'

He had a sense of humour. Now, that was a surprise. It was also disconcerting, it was...

*Sexy?*

No, of course it wasn't sexy. Gabriel Dalgleish was not sexy. Just because he was actually smiling at her, an oddly crooked and strangely appealing smile, and he'd rolled up his shirt-sleeves to reveal a pair of muscular arms covered with a light down of dark hair, it didn't mean he was sexy. He was stiff and starchy and probably performed sex exactly as he did everything else. Coolly, efficiently, mechanically, and yet...

'You can relax now,' he said. 'Doris has just left. Not that you'll be able to avoid her permanently, but at least you've postponed the evil hour today.'

'Oh. Right. Thank you.' She got to her feet awkwardly. 'I'll leave you in peace now.'

'No, stay. Talk to me.'

Talk to him? What did you talk to your boss about? The latest patient admissions, the crisis in the health service?

'I—'

'Annie was right—your name does suit you.'

'You mean, I'm a sandwich short of a picnic,' she said ruefully. 'I know I must seem like that to you, running away from Doris, but—'

'Not a sandwich short of a picnic, more…madcap.'

'That's an improvement?' she protested, and he laughed.

He actually laughed, and then she noticed something else. He looked exhausted. Sitting so close to him like this she could see that his eyes were bloodshot with fatigue, there was a very definite trace of five o'clock shadow on his jaw, and his normally immaculate black hair was rumpled and untidy.

How many hours had he worked this week? According to his roster he was supposed to work a ten-hour day but Nell had been complaining only yesterday that he was hounding the night shift.

'You work too hard,' she said.

'Jonah keeps telling me that.'

'Jonah's right.'

'Jonah worries too much,' he said dismissively.

What else had Jonah said? 'There's no room for failure in his life.'

Surely Gabriel wasn't insecure enough to think his whole department would collapse unless he was there? No, of course, he wasn't. He just arrogantly believed nobody could do the job as well as he could, and yet…

'Let's just say his family has a lot to answer for,' Jonah had said.

Had something happened to Gabriel in his youth, something that had scarred him, making him the man he was today? It would certainly explain a lot, and perhaps she should be feeling sorry for him rather than always angry with him. Perhaps she should…

*This is how you became involved with Andrew,* her mind warned. *First you felt sorry for him, then you made all kinds of allowances for him, and it was only after a lot of pain and heartache that you discovered there was nothing about Andrew to feel sorry for. He was just a rat fink.*

'Can I ask you something, Mr Dalgleish?' she said as he reached for the carafe of water on the table next to them. 'It's nothing earth-shattering,' she added, seeing his hand hesitate and his eyes grow wary. 'It's just... Call it curiosity—call it downright nosiness—but what makes you happy?'

'I think you calling me Gabriel might be a start,' he observed, and to her annoyance she felt her cheeks redden.

What the heck was she blushing for? He was simply asking her to call him by his first name, as any boss might do.

'OK, I'll call you Gabriel if you'll call me Maddie,' she said. 'And you haven't answered my question.'

'What makes me happy?' He thought for a moment, then smiled. 'Seeing a tiny preemie pull through against all the odds and eventually go home with his or her parents.'

'I can understand that.' She nodded. 'What else?'

'The neonatal unit,' he said, his eyes no longer wary but enthusiastic. 'When I was first appointed the staff weren't motivated, the equipment was ancient, and we were constantly having to transfer babies down south because there was no way we could treat them properly. Now we can keep them here, give them the best care available.'

'I can see how that would give you a sense of personal achievement,' she said slowly, 'but when I asked what made you happy I meant—well, I mean on a more personal level.'

'But that is a personal level,' he protested. 'There's nothing more important to me than my work.'

'And a cow is a ruminating quadruped,' she murmured, and he gazed at her blankly.

'A cow is a what?'

'It's a quotation from *Hard Times* by Charles Dickens. A little boy who has been brought up never to think of fun or fantasy is asked to describe a cow and he says, "A cow is a ruminating quadruped."'

He frowned. 'And your point is?'

'That just as cows are more than simply creatures with four legs who eat grass, life should be more than just work. It should be fun and laughter and dreams and…' She shook her head as he gazed at her, clearly bemused. 'You're right. There is no point, and I must go. My lunch hour is over and I have a stack of work to do.'

He nodded, but when she reached the canteen door she stopped and gazed back at him. He was still sitting at his table, and the frown on his forehead had deepened. He was a strange man, such a strange man. All arrogance and efficiency on the surface, and yet underneath…

A small chuckle broke from her. Unless she could go back in time and come back as a preemie, she was never going to find out what he was like underneath.

## CHAPTER THREE

'YOU said he was the boss from hell,' Nell protested as she sat in Maddie's office, balancing a cup of coffee in one hand and a crispbread in the other. 'You said he was arrogant, and overbearing, and—'

'I'm not saying he isn't,' Maddie replied. 'All I'm saying is maybe there's a reason for him being the way he is. Maybe something happened in his past—'

'Oh, God, this is going to be Andrew all over again, isn't it?' Nell groaned. 'Where's your biscuit tin?'

'It's on the shelf behind you, but—'

'Maddie, if you're planning on getting involved with a man like Gabriel Dalgleish, I need carbs for my lunch, not crispbread.'

'I am not planning on getting involved with Gabriel,' Maddie said in exasperation as her cousin lifted the biscuit tin down from the shelf. 'I'm only curious as to why he behaves the way he does, what might have made him the way he is.'

'Sheer bloody-minded cussedness?'

'Nell—'

'Maddie, you have a genius for picking the wrong men. Look at Andrew,' Nell continued as Maddie tried to interrupt. 'You fell for him hook, line and sinker, propped him up, massaged his ego, and then, when you needed his support after Amy and John died, the jerk took off, saying he couldn't cope with looking after somebody else's kids.'

'Andrew was different,' Maddie said, feeling her cheeks turning pink. 'I thought I was in love with him. I'm not in love with Gabriel Dalgleish.'

'You thought you were in love with Colin, too,' her cousin pointed out. 'Colin of the tweed jackets who was all intense and scholarly and kept saying brains were more important than beauty—'

'Nell, I was eighteen, a student nurse—'

'Until he went off on that archaeological dig and came back married to a pneumatic bimbo with the brain size of a pea.'

'OK, OK, you've made your point,' Maddie said with a shaky laugh. 'I have lousy taste in men, but Gabriel—'

'This is all my fault, isn't it?' Nell said. 'I asked you to loosen him up, to make him more human, but, Maddie, I didn't mean you to do this, to get hurt again.'

'Nell, I'm not going to get hurt because *nothing* is going to happen between Gabriel and me,' Maddie said with exasperation. 'We're chalk and cheese, oil and water, chocolate cookies and the Atkins diet.'

'You're sure?' Nell said uncertainly, and Maddie laughed.

'Nell, we'd kill each other within a week.'

They would, too, Maddie thought, when her cousin had gone. She and Gabriel had nothing in common. OK, so people were always saying that opposites attract, but she wasn't even attracted to him.

*You thought he was sexy yesterday in the canteen.*

Yes, but that had just been a momentary aberration, and she would never be foolish enough to act on it.

*You did with Colin and Andrew,* her mind whispered. *It was Colin's green eyes and air of complete helplessness that first attracted you to him, and with Andrew you took one look at his thick blond hair and his apparent total inability to deal with everyday life and you were sunk.*

Maddie sighed as she opened the database on her computer. Even she could see there was a pattern here. Maybe she belonged to a group of women who had been invisibly marked with the word 'Sucker'. Maybe women like her would be better off actively seeking out the biggest bastard they could find rather than deluding themselves into believing that the next man they met would be a prince. At least then the heartbreak wouldn't come as any surprise.

'Problem?'

She looked up quickly to see Gabriel standing in her office doorway, and felt her cheeks darken.

'Nothing you can help me with,' she said brightly, and he came forward a step.

'You may not believe it, but I'm actually quite a good listener.'

He was right: she didn't believe it. If she'd been a preemie with bronchopulmonary dysplasia and he could have put his stethoscope on her chest and listened to her breathing, she would have believed it, but listening to a fully grown twenty-nine-year-old adult? Nope, not a chance.

'If you're looking for the graph sheets on the incidence of jaundice in babies of twenty-eight to thirty-two weeks gestation, I'll have them ready in about an hour,' she said.

'Actually, I'm here because the new girl on the switchboard transferred a call meant for you through to me by mistake. There's a mechanic from McAllen's garage down in Reception waiting to collect your car, but you haven't left your keys.'

'Oh, damn.' She half rose to her feet. 'I'll take them down now.'

'If you give them to me, I'll get one of the porters to take them down for you.' He glanced at her overflowing in-tray. 'It looks as though you've got more than enough on your plate at the moment to have time to ferry car keys about.'

*And whose fault is that?* she thought as she delved into her handbag and began hunting for her keys. If he would only stop sending her off on pointless errands she might actually be able to get on top of her work instead of constantly feeling as though she was running very fast simply to stand still.

'You know, I read in an article somewhere that the contents of a woman's handbag reveal her true personality,' Gabriel observed, as she gave up on the delving and emptied the entire contents of her handbag onto her desk with a muttered oath of exasperation.

'Sounds like an article written by somebody with too much time on their hands,' she said. 'Oh, damn it, where are they?'

'Why in the world do you keep a screwdriver in your handbag?' he asked in fascination. 'I can understand the make-up, the spare tights, the hairbrush and the diary, but a screwdriver…'

'At *last!*' she exclaimed as her car keys surfaced. 'In case I need to unscrew something, of course.'

'To unscrew something,' he repeated, taking the keys she was holding out to him. 'Now, why didn't I think of that?'

He was laughing at her, she could hear it in his voice, and it was amazing how very different he looked when he laughed. Maybe it was because the laughter eradicated the arrogance which all too often marred his face. Maybe it had something to do with his oddly crooked smile, which made him seem strangely vulnerable, but whatever it was she couldn't deny that when he laughed he definitely looked younger, more human and decidedly—in fact, quite disturbingly—attractive.

*Red alert, Maddie, red alert. You've started to feel sorry for him and you're finding him attractive. All you need is to start propping him up and you're in big trouble.*

Swiftly she gathered up the contents of her handbag and stuffed them back in. 'I really must get back to work. As you said, I have masses to do. There's the graph sheets you need, and I have letters to do, forms to fill in…'

She was babbling, she knew she was, and with an irritated shake of her head she started inputting data, but when she risked a quick glance up he was still there.

'What's wrong with your car?' he said.

'There's an odd clinking sound coming from one of the back wheels.'

'Sounds like it could be a wheel bearing or a brake pad needing to be replaced.'

She didn't care what it sounded like, she just wished he'd go away. The longer he stood there the more she was noticing things about him—silly things, stupid things—like his hair wasn't actually completely black but had little threads of silver in it. Like his eyes were such a very dark grey they looked almost like granite, and like the fact—the very big fact—that he looked tired again, and she could feel an overwhelming urge to say, 'Come on, put your feet up, I'll make you a cup of coffee'.

*Ignore him,* she told herself. *Ignore him and he'll go away.*

'Incidence of jaundice in premature babies of twenty-eight to thirty-two weeks gestation,' she read, staring fixedly at her computer screen until her eyes watered. 'Worldwide studies suggest a marked increase in the number of male children who are…'

Faintly she heard a door shut and looked up. He'd gone. Finally he'd gone, but that didn't mean the danger was over. From now on she was going to have to avoid looking at Gabriel's hair, or his crooked smile. She'd vowed when Andrew had left never to get involved with anyone again, and she'd meant it. This weekend she was going to buy a dog. No, not a dog. It was cruel to have a dog and then be at work all day. She'd buy a hamster. She could relate to a hamster. They spent all their days running round in circles, too.

'Oh, Maddie, thank goodness you're here!' Lynne exclaimed, putting her head round her door, looking red-cheeked and flustered, and Maddie smiled.

'Where else would I be?'

'Well, Gabriel always seems to be sending you off places.'

So Lynne had noticed, too, Maddie thought grimly. She really was going to have to call Gabriel on it. One day. When she could look at him without noticing his smile, or the silver flecks in his hair, or…

'Private business.'

'Private business?' Maddie repeated in confusion, as Lynne gazed at her in mute appeal. 'I'm sorry, I was miles away. What did you just say?'

'It's the New Zealand embassy. There's some problem with my husband's passport, and they want me to call them back. Admin cuts up rough if we use departmental phones for private calls so I wondered if you could sit in my office and answer any phone calls while I use the phone in the communal staffroom.'

'Oh, Lynne, I really don't think that's a good idea,' Maddie said slowly. 'What if there's an emergency with one of the babies?'

'Nell's there, and a full complement of nursing staff. Ten minutes, Maddie—fifteen minutes tops—that's all I'm asking for.'

'Lynne, if Gabriel finds out he'll hang us both out to dry.' She thought about it. 'No, he won't. He'll crucify us.'

'He won't find out. He's gone up to Maternity to talk to Mrs Scott about Diana.'

Maternity was on the fifth floor of the Belfield Infirmary, NICU was on the fourth. It was much too close for comfort.

'I'd like to help, Lynne, I really would, but—'

'All I'm asking is for you to sit in my office and answer the phone. I'm not asking you to do any nursing.'

The ward manager was gazing at her pleadingly, hopefully, and Maddie chewed her lip. 'Fifteen minutes tops, you said?'

'Oh, Maddie, you're an angel.' Lynne beamed. 'And you won't regret it—I promise you won't.'

* * *

Maddie hoped she wouldn't regret it either as she sat in Lynne's office, gazing at the charts on the wall, the calendar ringed with the dates of staff holidays and the pile of infant progress reports in the out-tray. As long as nothing happened, they'd get away with it. As long as nobody arrived wanting to talk to Lynne, and Gabriel stayed in Maternity, they wouldn't be found out, but they were taking one hell of a risk.

'Hey, what are you doing, skulking in here?' Nell asked as she came into the office, and when Maddie told her she let out a low whistle. 'If Gabriel finds out…' She drew a finger expressively across her throat and Maddie shuddered.

'Don't, Nell. Every time I hear a door opening I think it's him coming back.'

'Look, why don't you join me in IC, instead of fretting in here?' her cousin suggested. 'Oh, come on,' she continued as Maddie shook her head. 'I bet you're dying to have a really good nose about without he-who-must-be-obeyed breathing down your neck.'

Maddie hesitated. She *would* like to look at the ward properly, see what advances and changes there'd been in an IC unit in the last two years, but…

'What harm can it do?' Nell coaxed. 'It's not as though Gabriel has forbidden you to go there. Good grief, he's always sending you to the unit on some errand or another.'

That settled it, Maddie decided. She really was going to have to call Gabriel on it.

'Maddie…?'

'OK, I'll have a quick look round,' Maddie said. 'But only for five minutes. I daren't risk any longer.'

'I don't think you'll need any longer,' Nell said, leading the way across the corridor and pushing open the door of IC with her hip. 'There haven't been that many changes since you last worked in an NICU.'

'How are the Thompson twins doing?' Maddie said.

'Ben's still on the ventilator, but we've managed to transfer Kieran to the infant flow driver.' Nell glanced across at her with a wry smile. 'You miss all this, don't you?'

She did, and in a few years' time, when Charlie was more settled and Susie was older, she'd like nothing better than to return to nursing, but for now… For now she knew the decision she'd made had been the right one.

'Has Diana Scott stabilised?' she said and Nell sighed.

'The ultrasound revealed she does have PDA. Gabriel started her on medication to try to close the blood vessel, and it seems to be working, but you know what they say about preemies…'

'Two steps forward, one step back.' Maddie nodded and walked across to the little girl's incubator.

Diana was such a cutie. Too small even for the smallest nappy, she had a little cotton wool ball nestling between her tiny legs to collect her faecal emissions, a tiny woollen hat on her head to ensure she didn't lose any heat, and her eyes were fused shut like a kitten's.

Maddie chuckled as she stared down at her. They'd have to be thinking of getting her a new hat soon, because the one she was wearing was already riding up.

'Would you like to give Ben Thompson his antibiotics?' Nell said. 'We think he may have an infection so—'

'You're giving him the antibiotics as a precaution until you can have the cultures tested,' Maddie finished for her, and Nell laughed.

'Once an NICU sister, always an NICU sister.'

'Looks like it.' Maddie grinned, but as she began to walk towards Ben Thompson's incubator she suddenly stopped.

*They'd have to be thinking of getting Diana a new hat soon.*

'Is something wrong?' Nell asked curiously as Maddie swung back to Diana's incubator, pulled on a pair of surgical gloves, put her hand through the circular aperture on the side and gently eased off the little girl's hat. 'Maddie, I said, is—'

'Where's Jonah?' Maddie interrupted, her eyes fixed on the monitor on the wall behind Diana's incubator where the graphs of her vital signs were displayed.

'In Transitional Care, but—'

'Nell, her fontanelle's bulging. I noticed her hat was too tight, and it shouldn't be tight when she was born only a couple of days ago.'

'Oh, my Lord—an intra-ventricular haemorrhage,' Nell exclaimed. 'Stay where you are—I'll page Jonah.'

Maddie had no intention of going anywhere. She'd seen this happen before with very premature babies. The vessels in their developing brains were very fragile and it only needed one to rupture for it to lead to an intra-ventricular haemorrhage—bleeding into the brain. Diana needed an ultrasound scan to establish how bad the bleeding was, followed by a lumbar puncture to reduce the amount of fluid, because if the bleeding wasn't stopped she could develop severe hydrocephalus, and all too often there was no way back from that.

Ultrasound equipment. Jonah would need to use the ultrasound equipment, and Maddie raced to the bottom of the ward and wheeled the machine back to Diana's incubator.

Lumbar-puncture equipment. Where the hell was the lumbar-puncture equipment? Gabriel may have sent her here often, but she'd always been so annoyed that she hadn't paid any attention to where the medical equipment was kept. Frantically she scanned the ward, only to jump as the ward door banged open and Gabriel appeared, closely followed by Jonah, Lynne and Nell.

'Nell said we have a possible IVH here,' Gabriel said, his face taut.

'Diana's fontanelle's bulging,' Maddie replied. 'I knew you'd want to do an ultrasound,' she added as his eyes fell on the machine, 'so I brought it over. I would have got you the lumbar-puncture equipment, too, but—'

'Jonah, I want an ultrasound, a.s.a.p. Sister Howard, I'll need our smallest spinal needle. *Move it,* everybody.'

They did. Like a well-oiled machine, the staff sprang into action and Maddie stood as far back as she could so as not to get in the way. She knew she ought to leave, but her eyes remained fixed on Jonah as he performed the ultrasound scan, and then on Gabriel as he reached for the spinal needle. Lynne had said working with him was an education, and she'd been right. Calmly, coolly he inserted the needle into Diana's tiny spine and drew off the excess fluid as though he was doing nothing more challenging than taking a splinter out of somebody's thumb.

'I want her started on phenobarbital and daily lumbar punctures,' he said, pulling off his surgical gloves and binning them. 'Hopefully that will stabilise her. If it doesn't, we'll try ventricular tapping. I don't want to insert a shunt unless we absolutely have to.'

Because once a shunt baby, always a shunt baby, Maddie finished for him silently.

'At least the bulge in her fontanelle was noticed quickly,' Jonah said, shooting Maddie a *well done* smile.

'Ah, yes,' Gabriel observed, turning slowly round to face her. 'I understand we have you to thank for flagging up this emergency.'

'It was just sheer luck,' Maddie replied. 'I'm sure if Lynne had been here she would have spotted it immediately.'

*Oh, big mistake, Maddie,* she thought, as Gabriel's eyebrows snapped down and Lynne gazed at her in anguish. *Mega, mega mistake.*

'If Lynne had been here,' Gabriel repeated, his voice suddenly silkily smooth. 'So where exactly was Sister Howard?'

Maddie glanced across at the ward manager but, from the abject terror in Lynne's eyes, it was clear she would never come up with a convincing story.

'She was—' *Think fast, Maddie, think fast.* 'She was in her office—on the phone—talking to—to one of the pharmaceutical reps. I know I should have called for her, but I guess—I suppose—my old nursing training just took over, and I…I…'

Her voice trailed away into an uncomfortable silence and she couldn't meet his gaze. Her excuse was feeble, pathetic. He would never believe her, not in a million years, and she stared at her shoes, waiting for the explosion to come. But to her amazement it didn't.

'As you've so rightly pointed out,' he said, 'you should have called for Sister Howard, but thankfully you're experienced enough to recognise the condition and to know what to do about it.'

They'd got away with it. She didn't know how they had, but he seemed to have bought her story. Before he could question her further she hurried out of the ward, thanking her lucky stars that her guardian angel had been looking out for her.

For the rest of the afternoon she kept her head down and her fingers on her keyboard. No way was she going to risk leaving her office and walking into Gabriel. All she wanted was for five o'clock to come, for her to be on her way home, so when her office door opened just before five and Gabriel appeared, her heart plummeted to the very bottom of her stomach.

'If it's about the graph sheets on jaundice, I've finished them,' she said, quickly reaching for the printouts.

'Good,' he said. 'What I wanted to ask you was—'

He came to a halt as her phone rang but, as she reached with relief to answer it, her relief very quickly turned to dismay.

'What's wrong?' he asked, when she replaced the receiver and began scrabbling in her handbag for her diary.

'You were right about my car. The wheel bearing and a brake pad need to be replaced, but they have to order the parts, which means I can't have my car back until tomorrow. I'll have to phone my neighbour, ask if she can look after the children until I get a bus home.'

'I'll drive you home.'

She shook her head. 'I couldn't possibly impose.'

'No imposition,' he said. 'You live at 19 Cornville Avenue, and I pass it on my way home.'

Maybe he did, but he didn't normally leave the unit when she did. In fact, there were times when she wondered if he ever left the unit at all or if he perhaps slept in one of the broom cupboards.

*Gift horse, Maddie,* her mind whispered. *Don't look a gift horse in the mouth, not when you know how Charlie freaks out if you're not there when he gets home.*

'Well, if it's no trouble…?' she said.

'No trouble at all. Why don't you go down to the car park and wait for me there while I tell Jonah I'm leaving? My car's the silver BMW.'

Nice, she thought, but nice didn't even come half way close to describing Gabriel's car.

'I ought to have become a doctor instead of a nurse,' she said when she slid into the plush leather passenger seat beside Gabriel, and saw the array of high-tech dials and switches adorning a dashboard that wouldn't have looked out of place at NASA.

'Is that a dig at the salaries neonatologists make in comparison to nurses?' he said, and she smiled.

'Yup.'

He laughed. 'Believe it or not, I think nurses are paid a derisory salary for the work they do.'

She believed him. Whatever else he might be, she knew he always said what he thought.

'By the way,' he continued, 'I wasn't fooled for a second by your cock-and-bull story about Sister Howard.'

She froze in her seat. 'Gabriel—'

'If you weren't an experienced NICU sister, I'd have nailed you and Lynne to the wall, but as you are I decided to let it pass.' He glanced across at her. 'You're obviously not only a very gifted nurse, you also clearly enjoy it, which makes your reluctance to return to nursing doubly confusing.'

'I explained why I couldn't return to nursing at my interview,' she reminded him. 'Charlie and Susie need me.'

'Not for twenty-four hours a day,' he said. 'They're hardly babies and there are some excellent child-care facilities available.'

There were, but it hadn't taken her long to discover that by the time she'd paid for child care she would be working for nothing. And then there was Charlie. He'd already gone through more than enough in his short life without him feeling that she, too, had abandoned him.

'A secretarial post suits me best at the moment,' she said firmly, but as he deftly negotiated the rush-hour traffic on Great Western Road and began to drive up Cornville Avenue, she suddenly realised she was facing another dilemma.

Good manners suggested she ought to invite him to stay for dinner to say a thank you for driving her home, but common sense told her it was hardly likely he normally had his dinner at six o'clock, or that his meal would consist of macaroni cheese, eaten alongside two inevitably bickering children.

'Do you...would you like to come in and meet Charlie and Susie?' she said, as he drew his car to a halt outside her house. 'They should be home in about ten minutes.'

Which ought to be enough to shock him into putting his foot down hard on the accelerator, she decided. But to her surprise he nodded.

'I'd like that,' he said, and as they got out of the car he gazed up at the two-storey red brick building and said, 'This is a lovely house.'

'You should have seen it when Amy and John bought it. I

told them they were insane, but John was good with his hands. So was Amy.'

'You know, with property prices soaring the way they are, you could make a very nice nest egg if you sold it and moved to something smaller,' he said as she led the way inside.

'No, I couldn't,' she said, dropping her front-door key into a dish on the hall table and ushering him into a bright and sunny living room. 'For a start, we'd have to buy another house and, as you said, property prices are sky high at the moment so after paying for the other house there wouldn't be any nest egg left.'

'But—'

'And even if an estate agent could guarantee I'd make a small fortune, I still couldn't sell it,' she continued. 'It's the children's home, full of memories of their parents. They've lost so much in their short lives, I couldn't take that away from them, too.'

'Which is all very laudable,' he said firmly, 'but sometimes you have to think of the economics of a situation. When all's said and done, it's just a house.'

*And a cow is just a ruminating quadruped.* Boy, but somebody had really done a number on this man at some point in his life, and it had been a good one.

'That sounds like the children,' she said, hearing the front door open and the sound of running feet. 'Charlie might not speak to you, but don't take it personally, and Susie will probably be in major strop mode, but that's just puberty.'

'Maddie, I have met children before,' he said with a touch of irritation.

*Yes, but I bet they were all in incubators and none of them could talk back.*

'Aunt Maddie, you'll never guess what—' Susie slewed to a halt, pushed her way-too-long auburn fringe back from her eyes, and gave Gabriel a hard stare. 'I didn't know we had a visitor.'

'This is my boss, Gabriel Dalgleish,' Maddie said. 'He

kindly gave me a lift home because the garage won't be able to fix my car until tomorrow.'

Susie subjected Gabriel to another assessing stare and he smiled back at her, all jolly and hearty and avuncular. 'Hello, Susie, and what's your favourite subject at school?'

*Oh, don't,* Maddie thought, seeing Susie's eyes roll. *You'll be asking her next what she wants to be when she grows up, and then you'll well and truly be marked down in her book of life as a complete dweeb.*

'Where's Charlie?' Maddie said to forestall him.

'He's here,' Susie said, dragging her brother out from behind her. 'He got a B for his story.'

'Oh, well done, you!' Maddie exclaimed. 'Was it the story about the dog with the three legs?'

Charlie ducked his head with a mixture of embarrassment and pleasure.

'His teacher put a silver star on it,' Susie continued, pulling a folder out of her brother's schoolbag and holding it out for Maddie to see. 'And she wrote "Excellent", too.'

'I'm so proud of you, Charlie.' Maddie beamed, giving him a hug. 'Really, really proud.'

'And if you stick in, Charlie, and work hard,' Gabriel observed, 'you might get an A next time.'

*I'm going to kill him,* Maddie thought as she felt Charlie's thin shoulders go rigid in her arms. *I don't give a damn about his past, or what hurt him back then, I am going to kill him.*

'I think your B is absolutely terrific, Charlie,' she said quickly. 'I think you're smart, and wonderful, and as a reward for getting that star I'm going to break out the triple chocolate ice cream for dessert.'

It didn't help—she'd known it wouldn't. All the shy pleasure and uncertain pride had disappeared from Charlie's blue eyes and in its place was the blank look she hated, the withdrawn look that always tore at her heart.

'Charlie—'

'I have homework to do,' he muttered, and before she could stop him he trailed out of the sitting room, dragging his school-bag behind him.

'I have homework, too,' Susie said. 'And as for you,' she added, turning to Gabriel, 'you're a jerk.'

Gabriel laughed a little uncertainly as Susie slammed out of the sitting room. 'I see what you mean about puberty.'

'That wasn't puberty,' Maddie said tightly. 'Susie was right—you are a jerk.'

'I beg your pardon?'

'Don't beg mine—beg Charlie's,' she said furiously. 'Why did you tell him that if he tried harder he might get an A next time?'

'Because he might,' he protested. 'If he got a B today, then with a little application he could get a higher grade next time. It's called encouraging children to aim high.'

'Or undermining and denigrating what they've achieved,' she retorted.

'Nonsense,' he said. 'How will Charlie ever find out what he's capable of if you don't encourage him to work that bit harder? My parents always told me when I got an A that if I worked harder I could get an A plus.'

That figured. 'Why?'

He stared at her blankly. 'What do you mean, why? So I could achieve the highest possible grades, of course.'

'For whose benefit—theirs or yours?'

The colour on his cheeks darkened slightly. 'Look, all I'm saying is children should be encouraged to reach their full potential, and you're not doing that with Charlie.'

She took a deep breath to calm herself but it didn't work.

'Do you have *any* idea of how wonderful it is for Charlie to be able to write anything at all?' she exclaimed. 'No, of course you don't. You just waltz in here, thinking you know everything about me and my family, and in the space of five seconds utterly destroy what it's taken me two years to achieve.'

'You're over-dramatising—'

'Why do you think I haven't worked for two years, Gabriel?' she demanded, and he looked uncomfortable.

'I suppose I just assumed—'

'That I wanted a holiday from nursing?' she finished for him. 'That I had a yearning to sit at home and watch soaps on the television all day while my bank balance dwindled away to nothing?'

'Maddie—'

'He was *there,* Gabriel. Charlie was there, in the car with Amy and John, when their car went off the road and hit the safety barrier. He was just six years old, and he saw the barrier break, saw it…saw it go straight through his mother, almost cutting her in half.'

All the colour drained from Gabriel's face. 'I didn't know. I—'

'He was in hospital for four months with a broken leg and internal injuries, but what was worse—much worse—was that he didn't talk for over a year. Not one single word,' Maddie said, her voice shaking. 'He just used to sit in a corner and rock. And then, when he finally started speaking again, he screamed. For weeks and weeks, he screamed.'

'But he's better now,' Gabriel said uncertainly. 'Recovered.'

'Of course he's not recovered,' she protested, wondering how he could possibly be so blind. 'I don't think anyone—far less a child—ever fully recovers from something like that. He copes. He has his good days and his bad days. On his good days he'll speak, he'll try to do his lessons at school, and on bad days…' She choked down the tears she could feel welling in her throat. 'He sits in a corner staring at the wall and nothing I say, nothing I do, reaches him.'

'I…I don't know what to say,' Gabriel said awkwardly.

'Well, that has to be a first,' she retorted, and saw a flash of anger darken his face.

'I think I've outstayed my welcome.'

'Too damned right you have,' she said, and for a second she thought he was going to say something—perhaps argue with her—but he didn't.

Without a word he strode out of the room, and she clenched her hands tightly to stop herself from running after him and beating him senseless.

How could he have been so cruel? She'd known he was arrogant and thoughtless, but to do that to Charlie…

'Has your boss gone?'

She turned to see Susie standing in the living-room doorway, and took a shuddering breath to calm herself. 'Yes, he's gone.'

'He's an idiot, and a jerk, and I don't like him,' Susie said, and Maddie walked over to her and gave her a hug.

'You know something, sweetheart? I don't like him very much at the moment either.'

# CHAPTER FOUR

'WE'VE been carrying out the daily lumbar punctures you ordered on Diana, and giving her medication, but it's not stabilising her condition,' Nell said as she stood beside Gabriel and Jonah at the little girl's incubator. 'The ultrasound scans indicate fluid is continuing to build up faster than we can extract it so it looks as though we'll have to start ventricular taps through her fontanelle.'

'I wasn't aware you'd recently qualified as a doctor, Sister Sutherland,' Gabriel said, and a faint wash of colour darkened Nell's cheeks.

'I was simply repeating what you said last week, Mr Dalgleish—'

'Then it's hardly stop-press news, is it?' he retorted, and Jonah threw Nell an 'Oh-Lord-but-it's-going-to-be-another-one-of-those-afternoons' look.

'Do you want me to schedule the insertion of the internal catheter for tomorrow morning?' Jonah asked.

'Of course I want it scheduled for tomorrow morning,' Gabriel snapped. 'When did you think I wanted it for—the first week in September?'

'No, but then, I'm only a specialist registrar and not a high-flying neonatologist, so I wouldn't presume to read your mind,' Jonah said smoothly, and Gabriel's eyebrows lowered.

'You're pushing it, Jonah.'

'Likewise, Gabriel,' the special registrar replied, and when the two men's eyes met it was Gabriel who looked away first.

'Why are Kieran Thompson and Ashley Ralston still here?' he demanded, striding across the ward. 'My instructions were for them both to be moved into Special Care this morning.'

'We did intend moving them,' Nell said quickly, 'but Tommy Fenton kept pulling out his IV line and Hannah Wallace—'

'I don't care how busy you were,' Gabriel interrupted. 'We desperately need IC incubators, so if any babies can be safely transferred to Special Care you move them when I say so, not when you feel like it.'

Nell bit her lip and Jonah's jaw set.

'Now, listen, Gabriel—'

'Have you started Ben Thompson on the bronchodilators and diuretics I prescribed?' Gabriel demanded, as though Jonah hadn't spoken. 'His last X-ray showed definite signs of lung scarring. It's inevitable with him having been on a ventilator for so long, but we want to minimise the damage as much as possible.'

'I was wondering if his failure to thrive might be due to something we're not picking up,' Nell said tentatively. 'I know nothing's showing up on his obs, but I have a feeling—it's nothing I can put my finger on—'

'How frequently is his oximeter going off?' Gabriel asked, and Nell frowned.

'No more than we'd expect for a preemie, so it's definitely not respiratory distress syndrome, but I still think—'

'You are not paid to *think,* Sister Sutherland, you are paid to *know,* and if you have difficulty with that concept perhaps I should be looking for your replacement.'

Nell flushed scarlet, and Jonah banged down his clipboard, his brown eyes furious.

'OK, that does it,' he said. 'I want a word with you outside, Gabriel.'

'I have a round to complete—'

'I don't care if you're scheduled to meet the Queen herself!' Jonah exclaimed, striding towards the IC door. 'I want a word with you *now.*'

Gabriel followed him with clear irritation, but when they were outside in the corridor Jonah didn't give him a chance to say anything. He rounded on him immediately.

'I don't know what burr has got under your saddle,' he said, 'but treating me like dirt because you're in a bad mood is one thing—I'm old enough and tough enough to ride your punches—but when you start in on the nursing staff—'

'Jonah—'

'I've had enough, Gabriel. Nell has had enough, Lynne has had enough—damn it, even the cleaning staff have had enough—so until you can start behaving like a halfway civilised human being again, we'd all appreciate it if you could take a leave of absence. Preferably a long one.'

'Jonah, listen,' Gabriel protested, but the specialist registrar didn't listen. He simply walked away, and Gabriel let out a long and colourful oath as he watched him go.

What the hell was wrong with Jonah? OK, so maybe he ought to have been a little more tactful towards him and Nell, but when he gave an order he expected it to be obeyed. Neither did he appreciate being told the blindingly obvious.

It was like Maddie, he decided as he walked out of the unit and along to his consulting room. She'd overreacted, too, when he'd made that comment to Charlie last week, and now she clearly regarded him as the kind of man who would drown puppies. OK, so he would have moderated his words if he'd known the child had been so badly traumatised, but…

*You shouldn't have said anything at all. Not to Jonah, or to Nell Sutherland, and most certainly not to Charlie.*

OK, all right, he would apologise to Jonah and Nell. He'd tell them he hadn't been sleeping well this past week, and they'd understand, but Charlie…

He groaned as he sat down behind his desk. If only he'd known about the boy. If only he'd thought before he'd spoken—but he hadn't thought. Susie had been staring at him, clearly deeply unimpressed, and Charlie hadn't even been looking at him at all, so he'd said the first thing that had come into his head. The first bloody stupid thing, and now he couldn't get Charlie's face out of his mind, or the way the boy had trailed out of the living room, his little shoulders hunched.

Perhaps he could buy Charlie a toy of some kind by way of an apology? Desperately he racked his brains, trying to remember what his parents had bought him when he'd been a child, but all he could remember were encyclopaedias and science books.

'Sorry to interrupt you,' Lynne said, sticking her head warily round the office door, clearly expecting it to be chewed off, 'but you're not forgetting the pharmaceutical rep is due this afternoon?'

Gabriel gazed heavenwards with exasperation. 'What time?'

'Late afternoon, I think, but I'm not sure. You'd better ask Maddie.'

She'd begun to retreat and on impulse he held up his hand to stop her. 'Sister, what would you buy as a gift for a boy of around…' *Make it vague, Gabriel.* 'Eight or nine or so. I was thinking of perhaps an encyclopaedia, or some sort of science or technology book.'

Lynne wrinkled her nose. 'My boys wouldn't thank you for a book of any kind, but they're not great readers. Maddie's nephew is eight, so why don't you ask her?'

Because at the moment she sees me as a cross between the child-catcher in *Chitty Chitty Bang Bang* and the Grinch who stole Christmas, Gabriel thought as Lynne disappeared.

Then forget it, his mind whispered. She's only a temporary member of staff so what does it matter if she hates your guts? In a few months' time she'll be gone, and then you can forget all about her and Charlie.

Except he wouldn't forget. Maddie had been right and he had been wrong. Praise mattered at any age, but it mattered even more when you were young. How many times had he rushed excitedly home from school, clutching his report card, only to have his parents pour cold water on his delight by saying, 'Well done, Gabriel, and we're sure if you keep up your studies you'll do better next time.'

For years he'd longed for his parents simply to say 'Well done', only to eventually realise they never would. All they cared about was being able to say, 'Our son, the boy with the highest number of A-Levels in the school. Our son, the youngest specialist registrar in Scotland.'

How could he have forgotten that? How could he have forgotten the desperate need he'd felt as a child for his parents' approval? But he *had* forgotten, and in one thoughtless moment he'd crushed Charlie's delight and pleasure just as his own delight and pleasure had so often been crushed. Somehow he had to make amends, but *how?*

'I hear he-who-must-be-obeyed is in a foul mood again today,' Maddie said as Jonah piled a sheaf of notes into her in-tray.

'I don't know what's wrong with him. I know he can be hell to work with at times but this last week…' Jonah shook his head. 'Something's clearly got under his skin, but what?'

Maddie wondered whether she should tell him she'd virtually thrown Gabriel out of the house after what he'd said to Charlie, but as Gabriel possessed all the sensitivity of a gnat she hardly thought her action could have triggered his latest bout of appalling behaviour.

'Something I can do for you?' she said instead, as Jonah

picked up the letter opener on her desk, put it down again, then began opening and closing her stapler.

'I was wondering—not that there's any hurry or anything,' he said awkwardly, 'but I was wondering if there was any chance of you typing up my report today?'

She gazed at him severely. 'Would this be the report Admin has been hounding you for ever since I started work here—the report you only gave me the handwritten notes for last night?' He looked crestfallen and she chuckled. 'I did it first thing this morning.'

'Maddie, you're a—'

'Lifesaver.' She nodded. 'I know. You keep telling me that. Every time you forget to keep your paperwork up to date, which is more times than I've had hot dinners.'

Jonah grinned. 'OK, they say actions speak louder than words, so how about me taking you out to dinner tonight to say thank you?'

She laughed. 'I was only joking.'

'I'm not,' he insisted. 'In fact, I've been meaning to ask you out for ages.'

Maddie's heart skipped a beat. When he said 'ask you out', did he mean as in a date? It sounded very much as though he meant that, but she hadn't dated anyone since Andrew and she didn't want to start again. Her life was too complicated, and dating meant involvement and…

'Jonah, I'm flattered,' she began, 'I really am, but—'

'You think it's a bad idea,' he said, his eyes fixed on her, and her cheeks reddened with embarrassment.

'No— I— It's just…'

'Maddie, do you like me?'

What was there *not* to like? 'Of course I do, but…'

'I'm only asking you out to dinner,' he said gently. 'Nothing heavy, nothing complicated. Somewhere like the Casio Antonio. The food's good, the atmosphere's not pretentious, and I know you worry about Charlie and Susie so I promise I'll get you home at a reasonable hour.'

He made it sound so simple, and maybe it was. Nell was always saying she ought to get out more, and she knew she would agree to look after Charlie and Susie in a minute, but…

'So, is it a yes?' Jonah said. 'Dinner for two tonight at the Casio Antonio?'

He didn't have a crooked smile. He had quite ordinary brown hair and eyes and, most importantly—in fact, at the very top of the list she'd compiled of qualities she wanted to avoid in a man—she didn't feel even the tiniest bit sorry for him.

'OK—yes,' she said, and his face lit up.

'Terrific. I'll phone the restaurant and book a table for us. I'm guessing you'd prefer to eat early—say seven o'clock?'

'Seven o'clock would be perfect. I'll ask Nell to babysit Charlie and Sus—'

'Maddie, Gabriel wants you in his office right away,' Nell said, looking decidedly harassed as she joined them.

'And both his intercom and phone have stopped working?' Maddie said caustically as she gave Jonah the report he wanted and he left mouthing, 'You're a star.'

'He has Simon and Rhona Scott with him, and he doesn't want them to hear what he's saying,' Nell said, and Maddie frowned.

'Diana's parents? Why does he want me to go to his office if Diana's parents are there?'

'I'm guessing it's something to do with Diana's ventricular tapping,' Nell said. 'Rhona and Simon are really upset about it and maybe Gabriel's hoping—as you were the one who spotted the intra-ventricular haemorrhage—that you might be able to persuade them it's necessary.'

It made sense—sort of—and Maddie reached for her notepad and pen. 'Actually, while you're here, Nell, I need a favour,' she said as she stood up. 'Could you look after Charlie and Susie for me tonight for a couple of hours?'

'Don't tell me Gabriel's got you working overtime already?' Nell groaned, as she led the way out of the office, and Maddie smiled.

'No, it's Jonah. He's asked me out to dinner.'

Nell stopped dead in the middle of the corridor. 'Jonah's asked you out on a date?'

'Well, it's not really a proper date,' Maddie said hurriedly, feeling suddenly quite ridiculously embarrassed. 'It's more a sort of a thank you because I typed his report so quickly.'

'I see.'

Nell didn't look happy. In fact, Nell's enthusiasm was positively underwhelming and Maddie said, 'Look, if babysitting Charlie and Susie tonight is a problem I'll ask Jonah to make it another night.'

'It's not a problem.'

It obviously was.

'Nell, you were the one who said I should start going out again,' Maddie pointed out defensively, 'and I thought you liked Jonah?'

'I do… I just…' Nell coloured slightly. 'I wouldn't have thought he was your type.'

'I don't think I have a type.' Maddie sighed. 'Unless it's for low-life scum who hurt me.'

'Jonah won't do that, but…'

'Look, is there something about Jonah I should know?' Maddie demanded. 'Like he's a serial dater, has a commitment phobia or a wife and twelve kids in Edinburgh?'

'Of course he hasn't,' Nell said irritably. 'He's a lovely man, but he hasn't had much luck with women, so…well, just don't hurt him, OK?'

Maddie stared at her cousin thoughtfully. 'Have you ever thought that maybe you should be reconsidering your engagement to Brian?'

'Whatever for?' Nell said, genuinely bemused. 'Jonah is a friend—a good friend—but I love Brian.'

*Are you sure about that?* Maddie thought, but she didn't say it. She never would.

'Good luck with the Scotts,' Nell continued, lowering her voice as they drew level with Gabriel's consulting room. 'Judging by the mood our boss is in, I reckon your biggest task will be preventing them from hitting him.'

That was Maddie's fear, too, but after just ten minutes of listening to Gabriel explaining to Diana's parents that their daughter's condition wasn't stabilising, she decided that the likelihood of them hitting him was nil. The likelihood of them not understanding a word he was saying, however, was infinite.

*For heaven's sake, simplify it, humanise it,* she thought as he talked about tapping and butterfly syringes, blood pressure and internal catheters. *You're confusing them, and they're frightened enough without you confusing them.*

'I'm a good listener,' he'd said, but listening involved more than simply hearing what people were saying. Listening meant interpreting the unspoken. It meant watching people's body language, being aware of the expressions in their eyes, so you heard not just what they said but also their unvoiced fears—and he wasn't doing that.

'This tapping thing you're talking about,' Simon Scott said eventually, white-faced and tense. 'Does that mean you think Diana could develop hydrocephalus—water on the brain?'

*Don't answer him directly,* Maddie prayed. This couple have enough on their plate without you adding to it, so don't answer him. To her relief Gabriel didn't.

'We're hoping we'll be able to drain the excess fluid much more frequently with a tap than we can with lumbar punctures,' Gabriel said, but Simon refused to be sidetracked.

'I was reading about hydrocephalus last night on the internet,' he said, 'and on the web site I found…it said babies with that condition often become brain damaged.'

Maddie held her breath. Gabriel couldn't lie—she knew he

couldn't—but she hoped desperately he would remember to temper the facts with some positive information. To her relief, he did.

'There's certainly a possibility of hydrocephalus,' he said, 'but if we can stabilise Diana, get her weight up to 1,800 grams, there's a good chance her condition could resolve itself.'

'But what if it doesn't?' Rhona said unhappily. 'She has this heart problem—'

'One thing at a time, Rhona,' Gabriel interrupted. 'And the medication we're giving Diana for the blood vessel seems to be working, so let's take one thing at a time.'

'I just feel so useless,' Rhona said with a sob. 'I can't even express enough milk to feed her.'

'There's absolutely no need for you to be concerned about that,' Gabriel declared. 'While breast milk is undoubtedly the best for newborns, powdered milk will give Diana all the nutrients and vitamins she requires.'

That wasn't what Rhona meant, Maddie knew as she watched the woman. OK, it was what she'd said, but all too often the mothers of preemies felt sidelined, marginalised, by the high-tech equipment and medical treatment, and they needed to feel needed, to feel they were contributing something to their baby's care, irrespective of how small that contribution was.

'Feeding your baby isn't the only thing you can do, Rhona,' Maddie said quickly. 'If you'd been able to take Diana home right away, you would have talked to her and sung to her, so why don't you talk and sing to her now? That way she'll get to know your voice, know her mum's there for her.'

'What good will that do?' Rhona murmured, and Maddie reached out and clasped her hand in hers.

'Rhona, the nursing staff can give care and attention, but every baby—no matter how premature—needs its mother, and if you sit with Diana you'll eventually know, even before the medical staff do, when she's stressed and needs to rest, or when she's ready to bond with you. Later on, when she's bigger—'

'What if there is no later on?' Rhona said raggedly. 'What if she dies?'

Maddie glanced across at Gabriel to see him reaching for a piece of paper and a pen. He was clearly going to give the couple a list of statistics outlining the survival rates of premature babies, but that wasn't what Rhona needed, not right now.

'Rhona, I can't promise you she won't die,' she said. 'Nobody can, but your daughter's a fighter. She's already been through so much, and yet she's still here, so hold on to that thought.'

'This is all my fault, isn't it?' Rhona said, tears beginning to trickle down her cheeks. 'I know none of you has ever said it, but if I'd waited—not gone to the private clinic for IVF treatment—my other babies might not have died, and Diana...'

Maddie bit her lip. Lord, but this was a tough one. All she could do was speak from her own heart and hope it helped.

'Rhona, I don't think there's anybody alive who hasn't thought, If only I'd done this, or if only I hadn't done that. Hindsight's a wonderful thing, but the truth, is none of us can ever know how things might have turned out if we'd done things differently.'

'But—'.

'You can't rewrite the past,' Maddie continued. 'We might sometimes want to, but all we can do is deal with the here and now, and Diana is receiving the best possible care. Mr Dalgleish is one of the finest neonatologists in Scotland—' *he's also the biggest pillock in the world, but we won't go into that right now* '—and if anybody can pull your daughter through this, he can.'

Simon and Rhona glanced across at Gabriel, hope, fear and uncertainty in their eyes, and Maddie wondered how she would feel if it was her daughter whose life was hanging by a thread, or if it had been Charlie or Susie. It didn't bear thinking about, but she'd meant what she'd said about Gabriel. He might have zero social skills, but when it came to medical expertise she'd never seen anyone better.

'Thanks for sitting in with me,' Gabriel said when the Scotts had gone.

For a second she wondered if she should tell him he really needed to work on his people skills, but decided against it. Things were difficult enough between them as it was.

'I'm sure you would have managed fine without me,' she said bracingly, but to her surprise he shook his head.

'How do you do that—get inside people's heads to find out what they're really thinking?' he asked, clearly bemused. 'Is it because you're a woman, and statistically women are more empathetic, can read signals better than men?'

'I think it's more a question of putting yourself in somebody else's shoes,' she said. 'Imagining how you might feel in their situation.'

He frowned. 'It can't be that simple.'

She shrugged. 'I've always found it works for me.'

He leant back in his seat and stared at her. 'I was right, you know. You are wasted as a secretary.'

She got to her feet. 'This conversation was boring the first time we had it, and it's not improving with repetition, so if you'll excuse me—'

'No, please, don't go,' he interrupted. 'I want to talk to you about Charlie.'

Her expression hardened, but she sat down again. 'OK, I'm listening.'

'Maddie, I'm so sorry for what I said to him. I ought to have known better—I should have known better—but I spoke without thinking.'

'I'm sure that will make him feel heaps better,' she said, and he bit his lip.

'I was thinking of buying him something, like a book or a toy by way of an apology.'

'I can see how that might ease your conscience, but I don't see it doing much for Charlie, do you?' she said, and he shook his head.

'I guess not. Maddie, I'm sorry.'

'You've already said that.'

'And I'll keep on saying it until you believe me,' he said. 'If I could take back what I said, I would. If I could wipe out my stupid, thoughtless words and the effect they've had on Charlie, I'd do that, too, but I can't. All I can do is to somehow try to make amends.'

'Yeah, well good luck with that one, Gabriel,' she said, and he raked his fingers through his black hair, making himself look vulnerable and uncertain and all the things she didn't want him to look.

'What do you want me to do, Maddie?' he demanded. 'You want me to grovel at Charlie's feet? I'll do it. You want me to tell him I'm a jerk, an idiot? I'll do that, too.'

'Gabriel—'

'What was it you told Rhona?' he said, talking over her, his voice strained. 'That everybody has thought at one time or another, If only I'd done this, or hadn't done that? Well, that's me, Maddie. I bitterly regret what I said but I can't take it back. All I can do is to try somehow to lessen Charlie's pain, and I can't do it on my own—I don't know how—so I'm asking you—I'm begging you—to help me, to show me what to do.'

He meant it. She could see the misery and guilt in his dark grey eyes, and though part of her wanted to tell him to rot in hell for hurting Charlie, the other part whispered, *You don't kick somebody when they're down, and this man is down.*

'I think what you said to Charlie was thoughtless and cruel,' she began, then held up her hand quickly to silence him when he tried to interrupt, 'but you're right, you can't undo it. If you want to buy him something by way of an apology, I'd suggest a game for his Game Boy, but I think what would help him most would be you telling him you were an idiot. Kids are great believers in fair play, and if you admit you screwed up it might help.'

He nodded, stared down at his desk for a second, then up at her hesitantly. 'What about you?'

'Me?' she said, confused.

'Do you forgive me?'

She didn't. It was too soon for her to do that. The memory of Charlie's stricken face was too raw, too vivid.

'I'm working on it,' she said, and he smiled. A gentle, rueful smile that coaxed a reluctant answering smile from her.

A smile that slowly faded when his eyes continued to hold hers and she saw the guilt in them replaced by something altogether darker, hotter, more disturbing. *Get out of here, Maddie,* she told herself as she felt her pulse kick up and every nerve ending she possessed spring into life. *This man could keep a psychoanalyst in work for years, so get out of here, fast.*

'I...I ought to get back to my work,' she said, trying to jerk her eyes away from his—only to find she couldn't.

'Must you?' he said, and she swallowed, hard.

Oh, Lord, but it would be so easy to like this man. Hell, she was halfway there already, but this time it wouldn't just be her who would get hurt if it all went wrong. It would be Charlie and Susie, too.

'I have so much to do,' she said. *Stop looking at me like that. Please, don't look at me like that.*

'Maddie—'

'The departmental report,' she continued desperately. 'Admin wants our report, and—'

'Maddie, I was wondering whether you might like—'

She never did find out what Gabriel was wondering because the door of his consulting room suddenly opened and Jonah's head appeared.

'*There* you are,' he said with clear relief, then frowned when he glanced from her to Gabriel. 'Are you guys OK? You both look a little strange.'

*Being suddenly unable to breathe does that to you,* Maddie thought, getting hurriedly to her feet. 'I'll leave the two of you to it.'

'Actually, it was you I was looking for,' Jonah interrupted. 'I've booked a table at the Casio Antonio for seven o'clock so I'll pick you up at a quarter to seven if that's OK?'

Couldn't he have waited until they were alone to tell her that? Now Gabriel knew about her date and, though she knew she shouldn't care, stupidly—irrationally—she discovered she did.

'A quarter to seven's fine,' she muttered.

'Terrific.' Jonah beamed, and, when he'd shut the door again the silence in the consulting room was deafening.

'I'd better go, too,' Maddie said, and this time Gabriel didn't try to stop her.

This time he let her walk all the way to his consulting-room door before he cleared his throat and said, 'So you're going out with Jonah.'

It wasn't a question, and to Maddie's acute annoyance she felt her cheeks redden.

'It's a sort of thank you for some work I did for him,' she began, 'and I haven't been out for ages, and…' She came to a halt. Why the hell was she justifying her acceptance of Jonah's invitation? What she did, and who she went out with, was none of Gabriel's business. 'Yes, I'm going out with Jonah,' she said, and he picked up a folder on his desk and flicked it open.

'I hope you have a pleasant time.'

There was an edge to his voice—an edge that grated—and her chin came up.

'I fully intend to,' she said, and walked out of his room without a backward glance.

* * *

'You were right, Jonah—it is nice here,' Maddie said as their attentive waiter took their order and she sank back into the plush red leather of their cosy booth to admire the vibrant landscapes that adorned the walls of the Casio Antonio.

'Anywhere's nice when the company's perfect.' Jonah smiled and she rolled her eyes at him.

'Flatterer.'

'I never flatter,' he said. 'You're pretty and smart—'

'Enough—enough,' she said. 'Much more of this and you'll have me believing you.'

'Good.' He grinned and she laughed.

'You know, I can't believe you and Gabriel have been friends for almost eighteen years,' she said. 'I wouldn't have thought you had anything in common.'

'You'd be surprised,' Jonah said. When their waiter returned with two steaming plates of spaghetti carbonara, Maddie folded her arms across her chest and said, 'OK, surprise me.'

'We both love our work, we both suffer from low self-esteem and we both have a burning need to prove ourselves.'

'I can believe you both love neonatal medicine,' Maddie said, 'and maybe—though heaven knows why—you both need to prove yourselves, but you'll never get me to believe either of you suffers from low self-esteem. Good grief, Gabriel is arrogance and rudeness personified. He crucifies his staff—'

'But if you call him on it—tell him how hurtful he's been—he's always genuinely horrified, and will do his utmost to make amends,' Jonah interrupted.

That was true, Maddie thought, remembering how contrite he'd been about Charlie.

'OK, if it isn't arrogance that makes him so rude, what is it?' she demanded, picking up her fork. 'Did somebody steal his favourite dummy when he was a baby and he's still making people pay?'

'The only way you'll ever understand Gabriel is by meeting his parents. Believe me, they are not nice people.'

Maddie put her fork down again. 'You mean, they abused him—beat him?'

'You don't have to hit a child to scar it for life, Maddie,' Jonah said. 'Have you heard of Letitia Underwood?'

'The big-cheese cardiologist?'

'She's Gabriel's mother, and his father is Charles Dalgleish, chairman and owner of Reay Technologies.'

'An even bigger big cheese,' Maddie said dryly. 'In fact, a veritable Stilton.'

'With not an ounce of love in either of them for anybody but themselves,' Jonah observed, helping himself to a roll from the basket in the centre of the table. 'Gabriel went through hell when he was young, trying to be what his parents wanted him to be. It was only when he started med school that he finally saw them for what they really were, and he still has problems, times when he forgets success isn't the be-all and end-all in life.'

Maddie frowned. If that was so—and she didn't for one second think Jonah would lie to her—then she would have thought Gabriel would have praised Charlie lavishly for his efforts, rather than mirroring what his parents had done to him. But he hadn't.

'Jonah, do you suppose Gabriel—?'

'And do you suppose that we could talk about somebody other than our boss tonight?' He grinned, and she coloured slightly.

'Sorry. You're absolutely right. No more talk of Gabriel.'

And they didn't. Instead, Jonah told her about his numerous nieces and nephews whom he seemed to adore, and Maddie regaled him with stories of some of the things she and Nell had done when they'd been student nurses, which had him laughing uproariously.

'I've really enjoyed myself,' Maddie said when he eventually drove her home.

'Me, too.' He nodded.

'I won't ask you in, if you don't mind,' she continued as they stood on her doorstep. 'Charlie will use any excuse not to go to bed, and it's a school day tomorrow.'

'Not a problem.' He smiled, and as she half turned to open the door she suddenly realised with dismay that he was going to kiss her.

Well, of course he was. This was a date, and you didn't shake hands with somebody at the end of a date. *Don't panic, Maddie,* she told herself. *All you have to do is close your eyes and relax.* So she closed her eyes, and tried to relax, and he kissed her, but apart from his lips being warm and gentle she felt absolutely nothing at all. Which was fine by her—she was quite happy with warm and gentle—but it obviously wasn't fine for Jonah.

Faintly she heard him sigh, and when he released her she opened her eyes to see him gazing down at her, half regretful, half quizzical.

'No zing, huh? No, please, don't apologise,' he added as she opened her mouth to do just that. 'I may not have much ego but even I would much rather you didn't apologise.'

'Jonah…'

'I've had a lovely evening. Thank you very much for your company.'

She'd had a lovely evening, too, she thought as she watched him drive away, but it was the kind of evening you'd have with a friend. Jonah was a nice man, a kind man, but he was right about the zing.

*I bet there would have been zing if Gabriel had kissed you,* her mind whispered.

No, there wouldn't. He was cold and arrogant, and treated people as though they were idiots.

*Yes, but he has hot grey eyes, and a smile that does crazy things to your pulse rate.*

'Which are two of the very best reasons in the world to keep as far away from him as possible,' she said to nobody in particular as she opened her front door and went in.

# CHAPTER FIVE

'ARE you and that man an item now?'

Maddie put the last of the breakfast dishes she'd been drying into the cupboard and turned to face her niece. 'That man has a name, Susie.'

'Jonah Washington.' Susie snorted. 'Sounds like some kind of old-time American Civil War general to me.'

'He's a very nice man,' Maddie declared tightly. 'A fact you would have discovered yourself if you'd talked to him last night, instead of disappearing off to your bedroom the minute he arrived.'

'So you will be going out with him again?'

'No,' Maddie said, lifting the laundry basket so she didn't have to meet her niece's eyes.

'But if he's so nice and everything,' Susie protested, 'why not?'

Nell had said the same thing last night. In fact, her cousin had gone on and on at such length about Jonah that Maddie had eventually lost her temper and pointed out that it was a bit rich for Nell to protest when she clearly hadn't wanted her to go out with Jonah in the first place, and Nell had gone home in a snit.

'Susie, sometimes…' Oh, heck, but this was so hard to explain. 'Sometimes niceness just isn't enough.'

'You mean he's boring?'

'No, he's not boring,' Maddie said. 'He's funny and kind, and interesting—'

'If it had been that other man—the dweeb who was so snarky about Charlie's story—I could have understood it, but if this Jonah is so wonderful then what's the problem?'

Good question. An even better question would have been why she'd gone to bed last night and dreamt not of a kind man with soft brown eyes, but of the dweeb with the attitude problem.

'Susie—'

'It's Charlie and me, isn't it?' her niece said suddenly. 'Jonah found out you were stuck with us and he's legged it, like Andrew did.'

'Number one, I am *not* stuck with you,' Maddie said emphatically. 'I love you and Charlie to bits and if your mother and father hadn't died I would have been the aunty from hell, driving you crazy with visits. And number two…Jonah likes children, and if I could go out with him again as a friend I would, but he…he…'

'He wants sex and you don't—or at least not with him?'

It was television and the movies, Maddie decided. That, or the fact that kids started sex education classes much younger these days, otherwise why else were her cheeks scarlet whereas her niece didn't seem even one bit embarrassed by the conversation?

'Something like that,' she muttered.

'But, Aunt Maddie—'

'If you don't hurry up, you'll be late for school.'

'But—'

'We'll talk about this later, OK?'

*Much later,* Maddie thought as her niece clattered belligerently out of the kitchen. *A lot later. In fact, hopefully never.*

A deep sigh came from her as she leant against the sink and gazed out of the kitchen window. Why, oh, why, had she ever agreed to go out with Jonah? Yesterday they'd been friends as well as colleagues, but now everything was going to be so awkward, so difficult, and the thought of seeing him again today…

Maybe she could call in sick. It was Saturday tomorrow and she didn't work Saturdays, so she'd have a whole three days to prepare herself. Except three days wouldn't be enough. Three months wouldn't be enough, and resignation wasn't an option. She needed this job. The bill from the garage had been horrendous, and there was the electricity bill due soon and a telephone bill, so she had to stay no matter how uncomfortable it might be.

'You're not leaving us, are you, Aunt Maddie?'

She turned to see Charlie standing in the kitchen doorway, and her heart sank. How much had he heard—how much had he understood?

'Of course I'm not leaving you,' she said firmly. 'Now, I've got your gym kit all washed and ironed—'

'I heard what Susie said,' Charlie interrupted, 'and I don't want you to go away with that man. I know I sometimes mess things up, do things wrong, but…'

'Sweetheart, I will *never* leave you,' she said, getting down on her knees to look him straight in the eye. 'You, me, Susie—we're a team.'

'But Susie said—'

'Your sister got it wrong. Nothing and no one is ever going to split us up.'

'Promise?' Charlie said, his bottom lip trembling, and she drew him close to her.

'I promise,' she said huskily, 'and now I have to go to work and you have to go to school.'

'Why?'

Another good question, she thought, putting her fingers to her forehead where she could feel the beginnings of a headache starting to form. Jonah would probably spend the entire day avoiding her, Nell would be frosty, and everyone at the Belfield would somehow know she'd been out with Jonah. In fact, the only person who wouldn't give a damn would be Gabriel, which wasn't nearly as comforting as it should have been.

'Because I need the money and you need an education,' she said as she helped Charlie into his coat.

'BP normal, heart rate a little slow, but not worryingly so,' Barry, the anaesthetist, declared as Gabriel stood waiting in the operating theatre beside tiny Diana Scott. 'Ready to roll whenever you are, Gabriel.'

'I've sterilised both a two-centimetre and a three-centimetre catheter,' Sharon, the theatre sister, said, moving her trolley of surgical instruments closer. 'Which would you like?'

*What I want is to know how Jonah and Maddie's date went last night, Gabriel thought grimly. I want to hear it was a complete disaster but the chances of that are slim. Jonah's personable, good company and has dozens of nieces and nephews so he knows exactly what to say to children. Damn him.*

'Gabriel, I said which size do—?'

'The smallest,' Gabriel replied quickly, feeling his cheeks heat up behind his mask and seeing Sharon exchange a curious glance with Barry. *Concentrate, Gabriel. Your mind doesn't wander when you're working. Not ever, so concentrate.*

'Do you want the smallest reservoir, too?' the theatre sister said, and he nodded.

'With the catheter and reservoir in place, I'm hoping we'll be able to drain the excess fluid using a 23-gauge butterfly needle,' he told them. 'If we can't, I'll have to insert a shunt, and I really don't want to do that until Diana's both older and heavier.'

He didn't want to do it at all. Once they'd inserted a shunt there was every likelihood Diana would have it for the rest of her life, and no child should have to live like that.

'I hear Jonah's dating your new secretary, Gabriel,' Barry observed as Gabriel made a tiny incision into Diana's head. 'The girl with the odd-sounding first name. Portland...Waldorf...'

'Madison,' Gabriel said tightly through his face mask. Damn it, one date last night and already the entire Belfield staff knew about it.

'Is that the girl who's Nell Sutherland's cousin?' Sharon asked. 'Smiley face, auburn hair, brown eyes?'

*Tawny eyes,* Gabriel thought. Eyes that glow when she laughs, and hair that isn't just auburn but has tiny flecks of gold in it, which you don't notice until you're standing really close to her. The girl who thinks I have all the sensitivity of a pig, and I'd give anything to correct that impression.

'That's the one.' Barry nodded. 'She used to be a nurse, but gave it up to look after her niece and nephew when their parents were killed in a car crash three years ago.'

*Two years ago,* Gabriel corrected the anaesthetist mentally, *and I've bought a game to give to Charlie. A game I could take round this weekend but I don't want to take it round. Not if Jonah is going to be there, as he probably will.*

'I hope it works out for Jonah,' Sharon said as Gabriel carefully began inserting the catheter under Diana's cranial skin. 'He's one of the good guys, and he's not had much luck with his girlfriends so I hope he and Madison make a go of it.'

'Look, could we have a little less discussion of my specialist registrar's love life and a lot more concentration on the job in hand?' Gabriel snapped, which silenced Sharon and Barry immediately. But it wouldn't stop them thinking, and it was all Maddie's fault that he now knew what they'd be thinking.

'Put yourself in their shoes,' she'd said. 'Imagine what you would be thinking if you were in their situation.'

*Miserable old bastard* is what I'd be thinking, he thought bitterly, or—even worse—*jealous old bastard.* And the trouble was, he *was* jealous. Jealous of a man who'd been his best friend for years. Jealous because Jonah would have kissed her, touched her, might even have... No, he wouldn't have made love to Maddie, not on a first date, not with her kids in the house.

But he might have.

'Are you ready for the reservoir?' Sharon said, hesitantly holding it out to him, and he took it without a word.

Three weeks ago he'd been happy with his life. His one concern had been the efficient running of his department, and then an auburn-haired girl had asked him to stare at her and his heart rate had kicked up in a most unexpected way. He'd tried to tell himself it was nothing. He'd tried to convince himself that he'd simply been very tired, but when the same girl had said she was working on forgiving him, and then smiled at him with lips that had looked soft and moist and, oh, so kissable, all of his resolve to stay celibate had suddenly gone right out the window.

'Are you going to be much longer, Gabriel?' Barry asked. 'Only Diana's BP's starting to fall and I don't want to keep her under longer than I have to.'

'A couple more minutes, and I'm finished,' Gabriel replied.

*In more ways than one,* he thought with a deep sigh. Even if Jonah hadn't asked Maddie out, he knew she would never have wanted to go out with him. Not with the man who'd hurt her nephew, the man her niece considered a dipwad.

'OK, that's it,' he said, stepping back from the operating table, rolling his neck to ease the tension knot he could feel there. 'I'll wait with you in Recovery, Barry, and then go back with Diana to NICU.'

Where, irrespective of how he felt, he was going to have to ask Maddie when it would be convenient for him to bring round Charlie's present, because he could just imagine her reaction if he posted it.

'It's a shame you won't be going out with Jonah again,' Lynne said, her normally smiling face pensive. 'He's a really nice man and he adores kids.'

'It wasn't a proper date,' Maddie said through gritted teeth, wishing the ward manager would just go away. 'More a thank you for some work I did for him.'

'You don't think you could have been a bit hasty?' Lynne continued as though she hadn't spoken. 'Calling it a day after just one date?'

Maddie counted to ten but it didn't help. Why did everyone assume she'd dumped Jonah? Nell last night, Susie this morning, and now Lynne. By the end of the day she probably wouldn't be able to find anybody in the Belfield who didn't think she'd dumped Jonah, and it was so unfair. She hadn't dumped him. They'd just sort of come to a mutual agreement not to go out together again.

*Oh, get out of here,* a little voice whispered in the back of her head. *What mutual agreement? He kissed you, got zilch response for his efforts, so why in the world would he ever want to go out with you again? He's dumped you, but he's too much of a gentleman to tell everybody that.*

'Lynne, about Jonah—'

'I have to run,' the ward manager interrupted. 'Diana's due back from OR any minute, and Gabriel wants to put a cast on the baby who came in last night—Toby Merton, the full-termer with the clubfoot?'

Maddie nodded, but she doubted if Lynne even noticed. The ward manager was already walking away, leaving her with nothing to do but remember last night and cringe.

Work, she decided as she booted up her computer. If she worked she wouldn't think about Jonah, but whoever said databases were engrossing had clearly never tried to work on one with a headache. By half past twelve her head was pounding, and she was just about to concede defeat and go to lunch when she noticed a young woman in a dressing-gown go past her office. There was nothing unusual about that—she often saw new mothers bringing their expressed milk down to NICU—but when the woman had passed her office for the third time Maddie got to her feet and went out into the corridor.

'Can I help you at all?' she said, seeing the young woman jump nervously at her approach.

'My son was born last night,' the girl replied. 'He was transferred down to Special Care, and the nurses in Maternity said… They said I could come down, visit him—feed him.'

'Of course you can.' Maddie smiled. 'Did they forget to give you the security code?'

The girl shook her head. 'I have the code, but…'

'But?' Maddie prompted.

'I just…' The woman looked at her helplessly. 'I just never imagined when I was pregnant that there'd be something wrong with my baby.'

'Are you Toby Merton's mother?' Maddie asked, and when the woman nodded she said quickly, 'Please, don't be worried or upset about his clubfoot. All that's happened is the bones in his foot haven't formed properly. It's actually quite a common birth defect, with boys being affected almost twice as often as girls.'

'But why?' the girl protested. 'I took folic acid before I got pregnant. I took all the vitamins and supplements I was supposed to take. I don't smoke and I didn't drink, and neither did my husband, so why did this happen—what did I do wrong?'

'You didn't do anything wrong,' Maddie said gently. 'We don't know why some children are born with a clubfoot, but Mr Dalgleish—the neonatologist in charge of our unit—is going to put a cast on Toby's foot today, and hopefully that will straighten it out.'

'What if it doesn't?' the girl said tremulously.

'In 50 per cent of cases it cures it completely, but if it doesn't then your son will have surgery when he's a little older.'

'Then he's not…he won't be…?'

'Left with a clubfoot for the rest of his life?' Maddie shook her head. 'No, of course he won't, so why don't you go along to the unit now and say hi to him?'

The new mother managed a smile and Maddie waited until she'd gone safely through the security door, but when she turned to go back into her office her heart sank. Gabriel was leaning against his consulting-room door, watching her.

*Here we go again,* she thought. He'd probably heard every word she'd said and was going to launch into yet another of his 'You're wasted as a secretary' speeches. But to her surprise he didn't.

'Thanks for reassuring Mrs Merton,' he said instead. 'Maternity should have explained it all to her but obviously they didn't.'

'They've probably been rushed off their feet this morning,' she said. 'I just happened to see her passing my office and guessed she must be worried about something.'

'I'm glad you did.' He cleared his throat. 'I've bought a game for Charlie and, as I'm not working tomorrow, I wondered if I might come round and give it to him.'

He wanted to come round tomorrow? But that meant she'd only have this evening to prepare Charlie and she'd hoped to get him used to the idea gradually.

'Of course, if tomorrow's not convenient...' Gabriel continued, clearly sensing her dismay, and she bit her lip.

'I didn't mean— I didn't say... What time do you want to come?'

'Would ten-thirty be OK?'

Ten-thirty tomorrow. It could have been worse. Gabriel could have wanted to come round that night.

'Right.' She nodded. 'Fine,' she added, fully expecting him to go back into his consulting room, but he didn't.

He stayed where he was, almost as though he wanted to say something else but didn't know how, which was crazy because he normally had far too much to say.

'Is there something else?' she said, only to immediately wish she hadn't, because he moved a step closer, and being closer to him was not a good idea.

Being closer meant noticing all the things about him she was trying to ignore. Like how broad his shoulders were, how thick his black hair was, what a beautiful mouth he had, and…

She sucked in her breath as his eyes caught hers. Oh, hell, he had that look in his eyes again, that dark, hot look. That look that made her heart kick up into her throat. But this time it was worse. This time she could feel a wave of heat rolling over her. A heat that made her long to reach out and touch him, to bring him closer to her, and he was everything she should avoid. He was Andrew and Colin all over again, and she'd done that script, and to go down that road again to certain heartbreak…

She backed up a step, unconsciously shaking her head. 'Gabriel, I don't… I can't…'

'Maddie, what's wrong?' he said. 'You're… Dear Lord, you're not afraid of me, are you?'

There was horror in his face, and she backed up another step. 'No, of course I'm not, but…'

'*There* you are, Maddie.'

*Oh, somebody shoot me now,* she thought as she glanced over her shoulder to see Jonah striding towards them. She'd managed to get through the whole morning without meeting him and now he was here, and Gabriel was here, and all she needed was for Nell to come out of the unit and her misery would be complete.

'I'm really busy, Jonah,' she said, hoping to head him off, but it didn't work.

'We need to talk, Maddie.'

No, they didn't, she thought. It would be much better all round if they both just tried to pretend that last night had never happened, but Jonah looked like a man with a mission, a man who wouldn't be deflected.

'My office,' she said, and to her relief Jonah followed her. But he didn't even give her a chance to marshal her thoughts. The minute she closed her office door he was off and running.

'Maddie, I know there's always a certain awkwardness on occasions like this, so I just want to say that I had a very pleasant time last night and I, for one, would be more than happy to do it again.'

'You...you would?' she stammered, her eyes flying to his. 'But—'

'As a friend, Maddie. If you're feeling low, and want to get out of the house for the evening, I'm your man. If you want some furniture moved, give me a call. If you need somebody beaten up, just say the word and I'll batter seven bells out of them. I mean it,' he continued as she began to laugh. 'Think of me as your helpful Aunt Elsie but without the dress and the handbag.' He frowned slightly. 'Although if it's for the beating up, maybe you should think of me as your helpful Uncle George.'

He meant it. She could tell from the concern in his gentle brown eyes that he meant it. If she had any sense she'd grab hold of this man, and never let go. He was kind and honest, and he would never hurt her, but it wasn't enough, she knew it wasn't.

'Jonah, you're a man in a million,' she said.

'But not the man in a million for you,' he replied, and she shook her head sadly.

'I wish you were, Jonah. I do honestly wish you were.'

'So do I,' he said, 'but we can't always get what we want in life, can we?'

*Tell me about it,* she thought.

'Now, I don't know about you,' he continued briskly, 'but I'm starving. How about joining me for lunch in the canteen?'

He couldn't be serious. 'Jonah, if we have lunch together in the canteen everyone will think...they'll think...'

'That we're an item.' He nodded, his eyes gleaming. 'So how about we confuse them a little?'

For a moment she hesitated, but what harm would it do? Plus she had a horrible suspicion that if she hung about debating the matter Jonah would probably ask Gabriel or Nell to join them for lunch, which would send her headache into full migraine mode.

'OK, you're on,' she said, and he grinned.

'I like a girl with spirit.'

It's not spirit I have, she thought. It's a healthy sense of self-preservation.

'Good grief, but it's busy in here today,' Maddie said as she and Jonah ate their lunch in the canteen and watched the queue at the counter getting longer and longer.

'What we really need is a new state-of-the-art infirmary,' Jonah replied. 'The Belfield was never designed to accommodate the number of staff it has now.'

He was right, but Maddie couldn't deny she preferred the homeliness of the Belfield's Victorian dilapidation, even if lunch hours could sometimes be fraught.

'So, you're hopeful Kieran Thompson might be able to go home in a couple of weeks?' she said. 'That should please his parents.'

Jonah nodded. 'He's doing really well. It's a pity we can't say the same about his twin.'

'Nell's not happy about him,' Maddie observed. 'She still feels something's being overlooked, but she doesn't know what.'

'I'd back Nell's gut instincts any day,' Jonah murmured. 'She has a built-in sixth sense when it comes to preemies.'

'She was the same at the Hillhead,' Maddie began, only to realise Jonah wasn't listening to her but frowning at something in the queue. 'What's wrong?'

'I never thought I'd see those two together again,' he murmured.

'What two?' she asked, swivelling round in her seat.

'Gabriel and Evelyn Harper. They were an item last year until they parted somewhat acrimoniously.'

Maddie pushed her empty lunch plate to one side and took a sip of her coffee. *Don't ask. It's none of your business... Oh, what the hell. You want to know, you know you do.*

'In what way acrimoniously?' she asked.

'She wanted to get married, he didn't.'

She obviously still did, Maddie thought as she watched Evelyn beam up at Gabriel, her long blonde hair glinting in the afternoon sunshine, her white coat clinging to her perfect figure.

'She's very pretty,' she said grudgingly. Actually, she was gorgeous.

'Smart, too,' Jonah said. 'The youngest orthopaedic surgeon in Scotland.'

She would be. No, that wasn't fair. Evelyn Harper was probably very nice, even if she was practically climbing inside Gabriel's shirt.

'So, Gabriel's the love-them-and-leave-them type, is he?' she said, trying and failing to keep the waspishness out of her voice.

'Nah, he just dates the wrong women.'

'Oh, yeah, right,' Maddie declared. 'The poor man just wants to have sex with no strings attached and all these unreasonable women keep expecting him to marry them.'

Jonah let out a snort of laughter which he quickly converted into a cough. 'No, he honestly does date the wrong women. He has an unhappy knack of attracting the over-achievers—women like himself who need to be the best at everything—which, of course, is a recipe for disaster.'

*And pretty well rules me out,* Maddie thought, *because he's always telling me I'm wasting my ability, my talents.*

*Yes, but, then, why is giving you those hot looks?* her mind demanded. *And they are hot looks. Hell, those looks could blister paint.*

'What Gabriel needs is somebody to show him there's life outside the hospital,' Jonah continued. 'Somebody who will encourage him to smell the roses.'

'I wouldn't say he looks as though he's missing any roses at the moment,' Maddie said tightly as Gabriel laughed at something Evelyn had said. 'In fact, I'd say he looks like a man who wouldn't much care if the entire world was paved over.'

Jonah sat back in his seat and gazed at her thoughtfully. 'You think about him a lot, don't you?'

'Only because we all suffer if he's in a bad mood,' she floundered, annoyingly aware that her cheeks were heating up, 'so it's best to be prepared—forewarned.'

'Uh-huh,' Jonah said with a look that told her he didn't believe her. 'Maddie— Oh, damn,' he continued as his pager began to bleep. 'No, finish your coffee,' he added, seeing her half rise to her feet. 'There's no sense in us both missing out.'

She wasn't missing anything, she decided when Jonah had gone. One sip of her coffee had been enough to tell her it was as revolting as usual, and even if it had been the finest cappuccino in the world, the last thing she wanted was to sit here drinking it while simultaneously trying not to notice that Gabriel was chatting up an old girlfriend. And he *was* chatting her up. Evelyn was hanging on his every word.

Probably because he's hitting her with one of his hot looks. She sighed, feeling her heart dip. The looks she'd stupidly thought he reserved for her. Well, maybe this was what she needed, a wake-up call, a reality check. Hot looks might set her pulses racing, but what she needed was stability, commitment, and commitment wasn't something a man like Gabriel would be offering to a woman like her with two children.

Well, she might be a closet masochist but even she didn't want to sit here and watch proof positive of her own stupidity. She'd go back to the unit, cadge a coffee from Lynne and see if there were any chocolates left from the box one of the mothers had brought in earlier in the week as a thank-you gift.

'Nothing beats chocolate if you're angry or unhappy,' Nell was fond of saying.

'Too damn right,' Maddie muttered as she left the canteen, and if she hadn't worked out yet whether she was angry or unhappy it didn't matter.

All that mattered was she had to start growing up. She was twenty-nine, for heaven's sake, and she should have realised years ago that frogs never turned into princes. It was time for her to grow up, and she was starting right now.

Gabriel swore under his breath as he scanned the canteen. One minute Maddie had been laughing and joking with Jonah, then a crowd from Haematology had obscured his view, and when he'd looked for her again she was gone.

'I'm sorry, Evelyn, but I have to go,' he said, cutting her off in mid-flow. 'I've just seen somebody I need to speak to.'

Evelyn said something in reply but he didn't stop to find out what. All he was interested in was in finding out what he'd said, or done, that had caused Maddie to back away from him in the corridor earlier, looking for all the world as though she was afraid of him.

Hell, he knew he had a sharp tongue and a brusque manner, but never would he have wanted anybody to be afraid of him, and especially not Maddie. He needed to talk to her, to find out what was wrong, but when he went out into the corridor his heart sank when he saw her standing by the lifts, surrounded by at least a dozen members of staff.

Sod's law, he decided when a lift arrived and everybody squashed in.

Definitely Sod's law, he thought as a chorus of voices shouted out, 'Fifth floor, please.'

If there had been any fairness in the world they would all

have been getting off at the second floor but, no, they were all, bar a couple of nurses, going to the fifth. Well, he might be stuck in a lift with an audience of a dozen members of staff, but that didn't mean he couldn't talk to her, he decided, forcing his way to the back of the lift where she was standing sandwiched between the wall and a portly porter.

'We should have taken the stairs,' he said, smiling down at her.

'Yes.'

Just 'Yes'. Nothing more, and she didn't even look up at him, but kept her eyes fixed on the safety poster on the wall beside her.

OK, he thought. Work. He'd talk about work, and see if that got her attention.

'Have we received any emails from a Duncan Lindsay this morning?' he said. 'I met him at a conference last month and he expressed an interest in publishing an article I've written on retinopathy in premature babies.'

'You have an email from Elliot Mackay of the Royal Infirmary in Edinburgh, one from the BMA, but nothing from a Duncan Lindsay.'

'I hope he's not going to leave it until the last minute to say yes or no,' he said as the lift lurched to a halt at the second floor and the two nurses got out. 'It's quite a lengthy article and I'll need you to type it out before I send it.'

'Yes.'

'Sometimes I think these editors don't realise we have "proper" jobs,' he continued determinedly.

'No.'

'In fact, they probably think we have nothing better to do than sit about all day waiting for them to ring or email.'

'Probably.'

*Oh, give it up, Gabriel,* he told himself as he stared down at her and realised she hadn't once turned her head in his direction. She's not interested in you—she's never going to be interested in you.

Evelyn was. Evelyn had made it abundantly clear that she'd be more than willing to resume their relationship, but he didn't want to resume the relationship. He wanted the girl standing next to him. The girl with the white face and strained eyes who was now staring fixedly at the lift buttons as though willing them to change faster.

'Maddie—'

'I'll see if anything has come in for you from Duncan Lindsay during lunch,' she said over him as the lift doors opened on the fourth floor and she pushed her way out.

'There's no hurry,' he called after her, but she was already hurrying away and he clenched his teeth with exasperation as he followed her.

She would never have dashed off like that if Jonah had been in the lift with her but, then, with umpteen nieces and nephews Jonah knew exactly what to say to kids. Damn and blast him.

'Gabriel, can I have a word?'

Only if you're going to tell me you and Maddie had a really lousy time last night and you're not going out with her again, Gabriel thought as he saw Jonah walking towards him, a broad smile lighting up his face.

'I'm a bit busy, Jonah—'

'It's about Ben Thompson.'

'What about Ben?' Gabriel demanded, all thoughts of Maddie vanishing instantly from his mind.

'I had an emergency call during lunch because he'd stopped breathing, and while Nell was waiting for me to arrive she realised his ventilator tube was blocked so she took it out, inserted a new tube and administered heart massage.'

'Is he all right?' Gabriel said, beginning to head towards the unit. 'The longer he wasn't breathing—'

'Gabriel, he was back to normal within minutes, and his blood-oxygen saturation improved even when his oxygen was reduced from 100 per cent to 40 per cent. The tube was blocked with five centimetres of debris and fluid from his lungs and my guess is it's been gradually building up over time.'

'So Sister Sutherland was right,' Gabriel said slowly. 'We were missing something.'

Jonah nodded. 'Smart girl, Nell. In fact, if you weren't so set on Maddie taking over as Ward Manager, I'd recommend Nell to take Lynne's place.'

'I'm surprised you're not pushing for Maddie in the circumstances,' Gabriel said, more caustically than he'd intended, and Jonah looked puzzled.

'What circumstances?'

'Well, you and she…' Gabriel's jaw tightened. 'You're dating, aren't you?'

A flash of anger darkened Jonah's face. 'Maddie and I are not dating, and even if we were, I would never allow my private feelings to get in the way of my professional judgment, and I take great exception to you suggesting it.'

'You're not dating?' Gabriel repeated. 'But you went out together last night, didn't you?'

The anger on Jonah's face faded, to be slowly replaced by a look of dawning comprehension. 'Maddie and I went out to dinner as friends. End of story.'

'I see,' Gabriel said slowly, and Jonah nodded.

'I think I do, too. And now I have a ward round to do, so if you'll excuse me…'

Gabriel muttered something in reply, but what he really wanted was to punch the air in relief. He had a chance now. OK, so it wasn't a very good one, and the possibilities of him screwing up again were limitless, but he had a chance, and he was going to grab it with both hands.

# CHAPTER SIX

'SO...YOU accept my apology?' Nell said, her face anxious, her eyes uncertain. 'For what I said to you on Thursday evening about Jonah?'

'Of course I do, you idiot,' Maddie replied as she took the last of the washing out of the washing machine and began loading it into the tumbledrier. 'We both said things we shouldn't have, and you're right about Jonah. He *is* nice. He's just not for me—not in a romantic sense.'

'I know.' Nell glanced up at the kitchen clock, and sighed. 'I'd better get going but I wish I could stay here with you—give you some moral support when Gabriel arrives—instead of going into work.'

It's not moral support I need, Maddie thought. It's to grow up. To stop being a walking doormat for men with hang-ups to wipe their feet on before they dump me.

'What did Charlie say when you told him Gabriel was coming?' Nell continued, and Maddie hit the tumbledrier's 'on' button with more force than was necessary.

'Nothing. He just shrugged.'

'It could have been worse,' Nell observed, watching her. 'He could have flat-out refused to meet him.'

'I know.'

Nell stared at her for a moment, then shook her head. 'OK,

what's up? I know you have the boss from hell arriving in half an hour and Lord knows that's enough to put a damper on any woman's Saturday morning, but there's something else—something you're not telling me. So give.'

'There's nothing wrong,' Maddie protested, and her cousin gave her a very hard stare.

'Yeah, right, so how come you're standing there, looking like you didn't get a wink of sleep last night—'

'Charlie was restless.'

'Wearing what has to be your oldest and tattiest sweatshirt and jeans—'

'I don't see why I should dress up for a visit from Gabriel Dalgleish.'

'Almost as though…' Nell's eyes narrowed. 'Almost as though you're deliberately trying to make yourself look as unattractive as possible. Why are you trying to make yourself look unattractive?'

'Nell…'

'He's hitting on you, isn't he?' Nell said, her face suddenly dangerous with anger. 'The arrogant bastard's hitting on you, and you don't want to knock him back in case you lose your job—'

'He's not hitting on me,' Maddie interrupted, then flushed slightly as her cousin gave her an I-don't-believe-you look. 'Well, he is—sort of.'

'What do you mean, *sort of?*' her cousin demanded. 'How can you *sort of* hit on somebody?

'He keeps looking at me. I know that sounds really dumb and stupid,' Maddie continued quickly, as Nell stared at her, 'but you know how sometimes you can meet a man, and he looks at you, and somehow you can't look away? Well, that's how it is with Gabriel and me. He keeps looking at me, and when he does, my heart…it does this stupid little back flip and I get… I get these weird feelings and thoughts about him.'

'Oh, Maddie, why can't you just feel fear and loathing like the rest of us?' Nell groaned.

'I don't *know,*' Maddie retorted. 'I don't know why he makes me feel the way I do, but it's OK. I can handle it. I *am* handling it.'

'By wearing your oldest clothes?' Nell's voice was heavy with scorn. 'Maddie, if you're exchanging hot looks with Gabriel, he won't notice if you're wearing a bin bag.'

'But—'

'What is it with you and your attraction to men who are users and takers?' her cousin demanded. 'You're smart, you're sassy, and if anybody hurt or upset Charlie or Susie you'd tear them limb from limb, but when it comes to yourself you're a complete pushover.'

'I know—I *know.* Which is why this…this thing between Gabriel and me—whatever it is—is going to stop, and stop now,' Maddie said firmly.

'You mean it?' Nell said, scanning her face. 'I know you must think I'm awful—sticking my nose in where it's not wanted—but I don't want you to get hurt again. I…' Her cousin shook her head, her eyes very bright. 'I love you, you dope, and I remember what you were like after Andrew, and I couldn't bear for you to go through that again.'

*I don't want to go through it again either,* Maddie thought as Nell reluctantly left for work. The minute Gabriel had made his apology she was going to show him the door, and then she'd take Charlie to the Botanic Gardens. Susie wouldn't want to come, since she'd developed a teenager's total aversion to sunlight and would spend the whole day holed up in her bedroom, listening to her CDs, but she'd take Charlie to the gardens and walk in the early June sunshine, and not think about Gabriel Dalgleish at all.

'The dweeb's arrived,' Susie called, and Maddie chuckled as she heard the front doorbell ring.

Her niece must have been watching out for Gabriel from her upstairs bedroom and it was just as well he wasn't coming to apologise to her. If he had been, she would have been scraping bits of Gabriel off the wall for weeks.

Got to be more like Susie, she thought as she walked down the hallway. *Definitely got to be more like Susie,* she told herself when she opened the door and saw Gabriel standing on the doorstep, looking sexier than she would have thought possible in a blue open-necked shirt and hip-hugging black cords, and more nervous than any man who looked as good as he did had any need to be.

'Am I too early?' he said, clearly misinterpreting her slack-jawed silence.

'No—please—come in,' she managed to reply. 'You're right on time.'

Right on time and she wished she was wearing something pretty, something nice, instead of looking like a bag lady.

No, she didn't. Dressing down was sensible. Dressing down was good, and so was the briefcase he was carrying. It meant he must be going on to the hospital after speaking to Charlie so his visit was going to be a short one. It couldn't be short enough as far as she was concerned.

'Charlie's in the sitting room,' she said, leading the way down the hall. 'He seems OK about your visit, but…' But not OK enough to have put away his construction toy as she'd asked, she noticed when she opened the sitting-room door to find Charlie sitting in the middle of the floor, surrounded by the bits and pieces of the bridge he was working on. 'Charlie, Mr Dalgleish is here. I told you he was coming, if you remember,' she added, when her nephew didn't lift his head.

'I remember,' Charlie muttered, or at least Maddie thought that was what he'd muttered. With his head bent over the model of the Golden Gate bridge, it was hard to tell.

'OK, I'll leave the two of you to it, shall I?' she said, and saw Gabriel's mouth fall open.

'But I thought—I expected—you'd stay,' he said, and she shook her head.

'I think it's better if I leave the two of you alone together, don't you? I'll be right next door in the kitchen if you need anything.'

She was gone before Gabriel could say anything. Gone before he could say, Please, don't leave me. What if I screw up again? And I just know I'm going to screw up again.

*Oh, get a grip, Gabriel*, he told himself as he stared at Charlie's lowered head. *You're thirty-six years old, not twelve, so stop standing here like a big dummy. Get on with it.*

'Charlie, I'm very sorry for what I said about your story,' he began. 'It was a stupid thing to say—a really dumb thing to say—and I was wrong, completely and utterly wrong.'

Silence was his only reply, and Gabriel felt a wave of panic wash over him. Why wouldn't the boy look at him—say something to him? Even 'Get stuffed' would have been better than this awful silence. It was all going wrong—his carefully rehearsed apology was all going wrong—but how could you apologise to someone who wouldn't even acknowledge your presence, make eye contact with you?

In desperation he opened his briefcase and took out a wrapped package.

'I...I bought this for you, Charlie,' he said. 'It's for your Game Boy. Your aunt said you liked games and I—well, I figured you could never have too many games.' Still Charlie didn't look up and Gabriel pulled the wrapping paper off the game. 'I don't know if you have this one, but if you do I can get it exchanged.'

For a long second he thought Charlie was going to continue to ignore him, then the boy lifted his head, stared at the game he was holding out to him, and said, 'I don't have that one.'

'And you'll accept it from me?' Gabriel said.

Charlie shrugged. 'If you want,' he said, but he didn't take it.

'I'll put it down here on the coffee table, then, shall I?' Gabriel said, feeling a trickle of sweat run down his back. Lord, but he was never going to dread fundraising meetings ever again. They were a walkover compared to this. 'Charlie, I…I truly am sorry for what I said. My parents…they never praised me when I was young. I wanted them to, but they never did, and I should have remembered how hurtful that was.'

'My parents are dead.'

Oh, hell, he was making a complete pig's ear of this.

'You must miss them a lot,' Gabriel said awkwardly, and when Charlie didn't answer he hunkered down beside him. 'Charlie, your mum and dad were very special people. So is your aunt.'

'Yes.'

'Maybe…maybe your Aunt Maddie might let me take you to a…' Damnation. What did boys of Charlie's age like? '…football match as an extra apology for me being so stupid.'

'I prefer rugby.'

'A rugby match, then,' Gabriel said. 'I could get tickets for one of the Six Nation Championship matches, and we could maybe go to a game next weekend—'

'The matches are all played in the winter,' Charlie interrupted, and Gabriel swore under his breath.

Of course they were. Could he get *nothing* right?

'Charlie—'

'I need to get this bridge finished.'

He'd been dismissed. Charlie might not have said 'Go away', but he might just as well have done.

*Well, what the hell did you expect?* his mind whispered as he picked up his briefcase and backed out of the sitting room. *That you and Charlie would end up having one of those big tearful hugs you see in the movies? This is real life, Gabriel, not the movies.*

'How did it go?' Maddie said the minute he walked into the kitchen.

He would have told her the truth—that he thought he'd

screwed up again—but she wasn't alone. Susie was with her, perched on the kitchen table, her brown eyes alert and watchful, and he managed a smile.

'OK, I think.'

'And you apologised?' Maddie asked. 'You said you were the one at fault?'

He nodded, saw her relax slightly, then her eyes fell on his briefcase.

'I thought you had today off?' she said, and he felt a tide of uncomfortable colour creep up the back of his neck.

He never used to think twice about dumping work on Fiona at the weekend, but now he knew he should have.

'Do you remember Duncan Lindsay?'

'The man who was interested in publishing an article you've written on retinopathy in preemies?' She nodded.

'I had an email from him last night, and he needs my article by two o'clock today so I was wondering... I know it's a lot to ask on your day off, but could you type it out for me?'

He saw the momentary dismay in her eyes, then she straightened her shoulders.

'Of course I can. How long is it?'

'About five thousand words. I know my handwriting's not the easiest in the world to read—' actually his handwriting was atrocious '—but do you think you can do it in time?'

'I could probably get it done in an hour and a half if nobody interrupted me, but...'

'But?' he prompted.

'What my aunt doesn't want to say is Charlie and I always fight if we're cooped up in the house together,' Susie declared, 'so a one-and-a-half-hour job is more likely to take three hours.'

Gabriel glanced across at Maddie. 'Is she right?'

'She's exaggerating,' Maddie said, shooting her niece a fulminating glance. 'I'm sure I can finish—'

'You know, I've just had an absolutely brilliant idea,' Susie said, making her eyes so big and innocent that all of Gabriel's mental warning lights ignited. 'If Mr Dalgleish took Charlie to the park, you'd be able to get his article typed up in no time.'

'*Me* take Charlie to the park?' Gabriel said, trying not to look appalled.

'Could you?' Maddie asked, her face hopeful. 'It would be such a help, and you wouldn't have to do anything. Just kick a ball about with him as you used to do when you were a kid.'

Which was fine in theory, Gabriel thought, but not if you'd never kicked a ball about in your life. When he'd been a child there'd been school during the day, homework in the evening, and at the weekend his childminder had ferried him to the library or a museum. Never once had he simply kicked a ball about.

'I don't know where the nearest park is,' he lied, and Susie smiled, a butter-wouldn't-melt-in-her-mouth smile.

'The Botanic Gardens are just round the corner, and I could come with you, make sure you don't get lost.'

'*You* want to go, Susie?' Maddie said with a look that told Gabriel that Susie wouldn't normally put one foot in front of the other if she could avoid it. 'But won't you be bored?'

'Of course I won't,' Susie said, beaming at Gabriel. 'In fact, I'm sure I'll find it very interesting.'

'Well, in that case...' Maddie said, and Gabriel pasted a smile to his lips as she reached for Charlie's jacket.

How the hell had he got himself into this? Gabriel wondered as he strode through the gates leading into the Botanic Gardens. When he'd got up that morning all he'd had to worry about had been apologising to Charlie and asking Maddie to type out his article. He'd pictured himself making the apology—successfully, of course—then he'd imagined himself spending the rest of the morning ferrying Maddie cups of coffee, perhaps laughing with her over his appalling handwriting, and hopefully, if he found the right moment, he'd planned to ask her out. Now he had a football under his arm, a small boy trailing disconsolately beside him, and a teenager watching his every move like a mini FBI agent.

'Why don't we go into the Kibble Palace?' he suggested as the great glass house loomed into view. 'I understand it has a most interesting display of exotic plants.'

'We know.' Susie sniffed. 'Aunt Maddie used to take us there when we were kids.'

*And now you're fourteen, going on forty-five,* Gabriel thought grimly.

'How about feeding the squirrels, then?' he said. 'There's a man over there selling nuts—'

'We know,' Susie said. 'Aunt Maddie used—'

'To do that with you when you were kids,' Gabriel finished for her. 'Look, it's a beautiful day. Why don't we just walk about the gardens, look at the flowers and trees?'

'Do you know any of their names?' Susie demanded, and Gabriel coloured slightly.

'Well, no, but—'

'I thought we were going to kick a ball about,' Charlie interrupted, and Gabriel groaned inwardly.

If he'd been asked to organise a game of football between a bunch of kids, he could have managed that. He would simply have picked two teams, set up some goals, then supervised to make sure nobody injured themselves, but how could you spend an hour and a half kicking a ball about? Nobody could.

Awkwardly he backed up a few metres, put the football he was carrying on the ground, then kicked it to where Charlie was standing. Swiftly Charlie kicked it back, and Gabriel returned it, but this time his aim went wide and it rolled past Charlie and came to rest at the foot of one of the beech trees.

'You're not very good at this, are you?' Susie said, her face contemptuous.

A hot flush of angry colour darkened Gabriel's cheeks. She

was right, damn it, but why was he failing—and failing so spectacularly—to deal with this stroppy teenager and her brother? He was a highly educated man, a neonatologist who had written three books on the care and management of premature babies, and yet when faced with Charlie and Susie he was as much at sea as a first-year medical student.

It was all Maddie's fault, he decided, striding stiff-backed to retrieve the ball. She'd given these kids far much too much freedom, far too much licence, but as shrieks of laughter suddenly split the air, and he glanced round to see a father pretending to be a gorilla for the benefit of his two children, he knew it wasn't Maddie's fault. Charlie and Susie were just two ordinary kids and yet he hadn't a clue how to deal with them.

Maybe it was something you were born with, he thought as he positioned the ball on the ground, something you knew instinctively. Maybe it was something you learned from watching your own parents. Whatever it was, he'd been judged, and found wanting, and it wasn't an experience he was used to. It wasn't an experience he liked, and because of that he kicked the ball back to Charlie with far greater force than he'd intended, only to watch in horror as it sailed wide, ricocheted off the oak tree to Charlie's right, banged into the beech tree a few yards in front, then bounced back, sending Maddie's nephew flying.

'Oh, my God, Charlie, are you OK?' he said, running up to him in panic.

'You did that *deliberately,*' Susie shrieked, fury plain in her large brown eyes as she knelt down beside her brother. 'I saw you. You *deliberately* knocked him down.'

'I didn't,' Gabriel protested, all too aware that people were beginning to stare. 'Charlie—Charlie, are you OK?'

'Of course I am,' the boy said breathlessly, shrugging off his sister's hands and getting to his feet. 'I'm not hurt—just winded.'

'Are you sure?' Gabriel said, staring into Charlie's eyes. His pupils were both the same size, and he was breathing a lot easier now, but even so… 'Look the Belfield's A and E department is just up the road—'

'I am *fine,*' Charlie insisted, 'but, boy, have you got a mean right foot.'

'I've got a mean right…?' Gabriel echoed. 'Charlie—'

'Can you show me how you did that? Managed to get the ball to bounce off those two trees?'

He wasn't joking, and Gabriel didn't know whether to laugh or cry. He could have maimed the boy and yet there was real admiration in Charlie's blue eyes, real enthusiasm.

'It was just a fluke, Charlie,' he said, but Charlie shook his head.

'No, it wasn't—I'm sure it wasn't. Can you try to do it again? I don't want you to hit me this time, of course,' he added quickly, 'but I want to see how you did that, then see if I can do it, too.'

'Well, I can try,' Gabriel said, reaching out to retrieve the ball. As he walked back to where he'd been standing, he saw Susie roll her eyes in an I-don't believe-this look.

'Oh, Aunt Maddie, I wish you'd been there,' Charlie said, his blue eyes gleaming, his small face alight with achievement. 'At first I couldn't do it—not the way Gabe did—'

'Gabe?' she interrupted, glancing across at Gabriel, her eyes dancing, and Gabriel shrugged and wanted to tell her he didn't give a damn what Charlie called him, but Charlie was still talking.

'The ball kept hitting just the one tree. It took me ages to get the ball at the right angle—'

'I know,' Susie groaned.

'But eventually I did, and on my last kick I hit the trash can, too.'

'Oh, wow!' Maddie exclaimed, as she took Charlie's jacket and hung it up. 'So my boss is a good teacher, is he?'

'The best,' Charlie enthused. 'You see, to hit the two trees what you have to do is—'

'Oh, *please*—no more,' Susie said. 'Anybody would think you'd split the atom this morning instead of hitting two scabby old trees and a trash can.'

Gabriel and Charlie exchanged 'Typical woman' glances and Maddie laughed.

'I hope you weren't too bored, Gabriel,' she said after she'd ushered Charlie and Susie off to change their clothes and wash their hands. 'I felt so guilty after you'd gone, landing you with both of them.'

'I enjoyed it,' he said. Well, he'd enjoyed kicking the ball about with Charlie and, if Susie's repeated heavy sighs had been harder to take, he'd survived.

'When did Charlie start calling you Gabe?' she asked.

'In the park. He said it was easier, much less—how did he phrase it?—much less stuck-up sounding.'

'It's certainly different,' she said, and he knew she was trying very hard not to laugh.

Lord, but she was pretty, he thought as the sunlight from the kitchen window illuminated her face. Not beautiful in the perfectly groomed, perfectly proportioned way Evelyn was, but warm and funny and good company, and he wanted her, badly.

'How's the article going?' he said, not from any great desire to know, but just to keep her talking, to keep her there with him.

'I should have it finished in about half an hour.'

'Can I do anything to help?' he said. 'Perhaps translate some of my handwriting for you?'

'I've seen worse,' she said, then a dimple quivered at the corner of her mouth. 'But not much.'

He laughed. 'Maddie—'

'I'd better get back to your article,' she interrupted. 'Help yourself to some coffee, and there's biscuits in the cookie jar.'

She was turning to go, and he didn't want her to go, not yet.

'You're looking very nice today,' he blurted out, then winced as she blinked. *Oh, hell, Gabriel, is that the best you can come up with?* 'I mean, you look very...' *Say pretty, damn it.* But he didn't want her to back away from him the way she had in the hospital. 'Very summery.'

'Summery?' she repeated, glancing down at herself, then up at him in clear disbelief.

In truth, he hadn't even registered what she was wearing, just that her curly hair looked even curlier than normal as though she'd been running her fingers through it—*I want to do that.* And there was a smear of ink on her cheek—*let me wipe it off for you, let me touch you...*

'Maddie, I was wondering if you might like to go—'

'I'm starving,' Susie said as she bounced into the kitchen. 'What's for lunch?'

Maddie looked conscience-stricken. 'Oh, Susie, I forgot all about lunch. Give me a few minutes. I'll put something in the oven—'

'But that will take ages, and you'll have to stop typing, and Mr Dalgleish wants his article by two o'clock,' her niece said.

'It won't take me *ages,* Susie,' Maddie protested. 'I'll have a look in the freezer—'

'I have an idea,' Susie interrupted with a look Gabriel was beginning to recognise and dread. 'How about if Mr Dalgleish makes us lunch and then you can get on with his typing?'

'Don't be ridiculous, Susie!' Maddie exclaimed. 'I can't ask Mr Dalgleish to make you lunch.'

Just as well, Gabriel thought, because he couldn't cook, had never needed to know how to. If he was hungry he simply ate in the hospital canteen, or at a restaurant.

'We'll get something delivered,' Maddie said firmly. 'Gabriel, would you mind organising it? You'll find some telephone numbers on the cork board.'

'Not a problem,' he said, and was rewarded with a smile from Maddie before she hurried back to her computer. 'OK, Susie,' he continued, 'how about chicken biryani for four?'

'I'm a vegetarian. That means I don't eat meat,' she said, for all the world as though he was a halfwit. 'And Charlie doesn't like rice.'

'Pizza, then?' Gabriel suggested.

'Aunt Maddie makes wonderful pizza, but she makes it the proper Italian way, kneading the dough and everything.'

'That's good to know, but we're having take-away,' he said.

'I wouldn't have thought you'd have considered take-aways very healthy,' Susie observed. 'I mean, you don't know what they put in them, do you?'

*In your case, hopefully arsenic,* he thought, reaching for the phone.

'That was really lovely,' Maddie said, pushing the remains of her pizza away, knowing if she ate another bite the button on her jeans would most certainly pop. 'But you must let me reimburse you.'

Gabriel smiled. 'My treat. It's the least I can do after making you work on a Saturday.'

'I didn't work—I had fun,' Charlie said, beaming, and Maddie laughed.

'He's a good kid,' Gabriel said, when Charlie had dashed off to examine the game he'd given him, and Maddie had persuaded a clearly reluctant Susie that she really should phone the friend who had left a message for her while she'd been out.

'They both are,' Maddie said, as she began clearing the kitchen table. 'I know Susie can be a bit difficult at times, but her heart's in the right place.'

Something about his expression told her he didn't agree, and Maddie wondered what her niece could have said or done to get under his skin while they'd been in the Botanic

Gardens, but she didn't ask. Don't invite trouble, her mother used to say, and on this occasion she suspected her mother had been right.

'I owe you big time for what you did with Charlie,' she said instead. 'I haven't seen him so happy in years.'

'Maybe I should patent the idea,' he observed. 'The way to a child's heart is to almost maim them.'

She chuckled. 'He didn't seem to mind, and whatever makes Charlie happy makes me happy.'

'Is that the only thing that does?'

'The only thing that does what?' she said in confusion.

'You asked me once what made me happy, so what else—apart from Charlie being happy—makes you happy?'

'Oh, Susie not complaining, sunny days, peace and quiet,' she said lightly, but he clearly wasn't satisfied.

'Don't you sometimes get a little lonely?' he said. 'Feel the need for something—somebody—else in your life?'

Of course she did. There were days when she would have given anything to have another adult in the house—somebody to talk over the day's problems with, somebody to share her worries with—but she knew that wasn't what he meant. He meant sex, and no way was she going to talk about sex with Gabriel Dalgleish.

'You obviously don't have children yourself or you'd know that loneliness isn't a problem, it's finding some time for yourself,' she said. 'Now, would you like me to email your article for you, or would you prefer me to copy it to a CD so you can send it yourself?'

'If you can email it for me that would be terrific, but what I'd really like is for us to start dating.'

*To start dating?* For a second she was certain she must have misheard him, but the way his eyes were fixed on hers told her she hadn't.

'But I thought you and Evelyn… I thought you and she…'

'Ancient history.'

Were they? She didn't know, and to her dismay she suddenly realised she didn't care and that was bad, seriously bad.

'I don't date,' she said firmly, and saw his eyebrows rise.

'You went out with Jonah.'

'That was different,' she floundered. And it was. When she'd gone out with Jonah she hadn't thought of it as a date because Jonah didn't make her feel the way the man standing in front of her did—nervous and expectant and, oh, so very much alive. 'Gabriel—'

'Maddie, do you like me?'

Jonah had said that, word for word, and she couldn't help but remember how their date had ended, with him feeling hurt, and her feeling mortified.

'That's not the point.'

'I think it's very much the point,' he said softly. 'Look, would it be so very wrong for us to go out together, to spend time learning more about one another, and see what happens?'

*Yes, oh, yes, it would be wrong.* Nell would have her certified, and the staff at the Belfield…

'Gabriel, you know what the Belfield is like,' she protested. 'If we start dating there'll be talk, rumour.'

'I don't care.'

*Neither do I,* a little voice whispered in her head, and though she tried to shut up the little voice it wouldn't stay silent. She wanted to go out with him, she wanted to spend time with him, and suddenly she realised there was a way she could do it. A way they could spend time together without it leading to recriminations, accusations, later.

'OK, I'll go out with you,' she said, but as his face lit up she added swiftly, 'but you have to understand that I'm not a single woman with no commitments or attachments. Charlie and Susie come as part of the package, so if you want to get to know me better, you have to get to know them better, too.'

'Not a problem,' Gabriel said. 'So how about the two of us take in a movie and a meal next Saturday?'

'Gabriel, you haven't listened to what I said,' she said gently. 'I'll go out with you next Saturday, but when we go out I want to take Charlie and Susie with us.'

'You want me to take your kids along on our date?' he exclaimed, his jaw dropping. 'But I thought—'

'I know what you thought,' she said, 'but Charlie and Susie are the most important people in my world. There may be room in that world for you—I don't know yet. But when you take on me, you take on them, too, and if you're not happy about that you'd better walk away now.'

He stared down at her silently, and she wondered what he was thinking. Probably trying to figure out how he could tell her he'd changed his mind. Well, it would hurt, but it was better to be hurt now rather than later. Better for them both to know the score right from the start, and when he cleared his throat she got ready to say, *It's OK, I understand.* But she didn't need to.

He smiled, that slightly crooked smile which always set her pulses racing, and said, 'I'm not walking anywhere, Maddie.'

# CHAPTER SEVEN

'IT'S like Gabriel's had a personality transplant, or something,' Lynne said, holding out a cup of coffee to Maddie, while Jonah and Nell helped themselves to a biscuit from the tin on her desk. 'Every time he's met me in the corridor this week he's smiled at me, and yesterday, when I dropped a syringe in IC, he said—now, get this, folks—he said, "Accidents will happen."'

'Maybe he's got another job,' Nell observed. 'He didn't come in to work last Saturday, and he never takes a day off, so maybe he went for an interview and has been offered some high-powered consultancy post in another hospital.'

'You reckon?' Lynne said, her eyes lighting up. 'Maddie, has Gabriel received any official-looking emails or letters this week?'

'Nothing that I've seen,' Maddie replied, taking a deep gulp of her coffee and wishing Lynne would change the subject. 'Just the usual queries, referrals, things like that.'

'Damn. That puts the kibosh on a new job,' Lynne said, then swivelled round in her seat towards Jonah. 'You know him better than we do, Jonah. Have you any idea why he's suddenly become Mr Geniality?'

'The good weather we've been having has scrambled his brains?' he suggested. Nell and Lynne laughed, and Maddie tried to laugh, too, but it wasn't easy when Jonah's eyes were fixed thoughtfully on her.

How much did he know? How much had Gabriel told him?

She'd made Gabriel promise not to tell anybody about their date tomorrow, but Jonah was his best friend, so he might not have thought he counted. Or, then again, maybe she'd got it all wrong, and Jonah didn't know anything at all, and was merely gazing in her direction because there wasn't much else to look at in Lynne's small office.

'You're awfully quiet this afternoon, Maddie,' Lynne said curiously. 'Something wrong?'

*Apart from the fact I'm becoming paranoid?*

'I'm fine,' Maddie said, putting as much brightness into her voice as she could. 'It's just been a long week.'

A very long week. A week during which she'd lied to Nell—*No, of course Gabriel won't be coming round to my house again, Nell*—and Susie and Charlie had fought non-stop.

'He ruined last Saturday for us,' Susie had exclaimed when she'd told her about the proposed day out, 'so why do we have to be stuck with the dumbass again?'

'Gabe is not a dumbass,' Charlie had retorted, his little face enraged. 'He might sometimes say stupid things, but he always says sorry afterwards, so he's not a dumbass. You are.'

And Maddie had tried to calm everything down without success and now she was seriously wondering whether she should just tell Gabriel to forget the whole thing.

Except she didn't want to forget it. She still wanted to go out with him. Even though she was getting nothing but grief at home, and Nell would hit the roof when she found out, she still wanted to go out with Gabriel.

*Maddie, you're not paranoid, you're crazy.*

'Yikes, is that the time?' Lynne exclaimed, getting quickly to her feet. 'We've got to get back to work, Nell.'

'Either I'm getting older, or our coffee-breaks are getting shorter,' Nell protested.

Maddie wished they were shorter for all staff when Nell and

Lynne hurried away while Jonah stayed resolutely where he was, clearly going nowhere.

'I'd better be getting back to work, too,' she said, gulping down her coffee so fast that her eyes watered. 'Admin wants our monthly through-put figures by this evening, and—'

'You're never going to keep it a secret, you know,' Jonah interrupted. 'Not in this place.'

Maddie opened her mouth, then closed it again. 'I…I don't know what you're talking about,' she said, and he grinned.

'Nice try, Maddie, but I've seen the way Gabriel's been looking at you all week when he thinks nobody's watching.'

She gave up on pretence. 'Please, don't tell anybody, Jonah. It's our first date tomorrow, and I want to keep it quiet for as long as possible.'

'Yeah, well, good luck with that one,' he said, 'but you might advise Gabriel to tone down his Mr Geniality act, because if I've sussed out what's going on, it won't be long before everybody else does.'

She bit her lip. 'I know.'

'I hope it works out for you—I really do,' he continued, 'but…'

'But?' she prompted, and he sighed.

'Gabriel's my oldest friend, but he's not the easiest man in the world to understand, and he has absolutely no experience of children.'

'I know, which is why I've told him we have to take it slowly,' she said. 'That he has to get to know Charlie and Susie as well as me, so he's taking us all to Pollok House tomorrow.'

'Gabriel's taking your kids out with you on your first date?' Jonah spluttered, laughter plain in his eyes. 'That should be…interesting.'

Interesting was the understatement of the year, Maddie decided as she made her escape. Potentially explosive was closer to the mark.

* * *

'I have Ashley Ralston's and Toby Merton's discharge forms here for you to sign, Mr Dalgleish,' Nell said, putting the slips down on Gabriel's desk.

'Has Toby been given an appointment to return to have his cast removed?' Gabriel asked, and Nell nodded.

'Maddie's booked him in. Oh, and Mr and Mrs Scott would like a word with you some time this afternoon, if you can spare the time.'

He could, but he didn't want to. Simon and Rhona wanted optimistic certainties from him, and he couldn't give them any—nobody could. The blunt facts were that only a quarter of babies born at twenty-four weeks survived, and of that quarter almost half grew up with severe physical and mental problems. Whether Diana would die, be disabled in some way or grow up to become a hale and hearty adult depended upon so many factors that were outside his control, but the Scotts wouldn't want to know that. He knew they wouldn't.

'Are you OK, Mr Dalgleish?' Nell asked hesitantly, and he managed a smile.

No, he wasn't. For the first time in his life he wanted to play hookey. For the first time since he'd achieved his goal of becoming the youngest neonatologist in the country he wanted to go somewhere—anywhere—where he wouldn't have to think about distraught parents or critically ill babies. And that was so unlike him. Once he would have described his work as challenging, fulfilling, but now… Now he felt restless, dissatisfied, and he didn't know why.

'Mr Dalgleish?'

Nell's eyes were on him, concerned, perplexed, and he frowned.

'How long have you worked for me, Sister Sutherland?'

Nell blinked. 'Three years, sir.'

'And you're still calling me Mr Dalgleish, or sir, and I'm still calling you Sister Sutherland.' He sighed. 'It's not right, is it?'

'Well, you're my boss, sir,' Nell said awkwardly, and Gabriel shook his head.

'You should be calling me Gabriel, and I should be calling you Nell.'

'If you say so, sir,' Nell said, then blurted out, 'Are you quite sure you're all right, Mr Dalgleish?'

'The name's Gabriel, Nell,' he replied, 'and, I'm fine. It's just been a long week.'

A very long week. A week when he'd tried to concentrate on his work, but his mind had kept wandering off to his date with Maddie, and that wasn't like him either. He'd dated plenty of women in the past, made love to quite a few of them, too, and yet none of them had managed to creep into his thoughts as constantly as Maddie had.

'So, will I tell Mr and Mrs Scott you can see them this afternoon?' Nell asked, and he sighed inwardly and nodded.

He'd have to see them—he couldn't put them off—but thank God he was going out with Maddie tomorrow. OK, so he wasn't happy with her let's-all-go-out-like-one-big-happy-family scenario but if she wanted to impose some kind of test, he could live with it, and if he got through tomorrow without upsetting Charlie or Susie he could start dating her properly.

And that was what he needed, he decided as Nell hurried away and he went out into the corridor to find Maddie taking a photograph of Mr and Mrs. Ralston with their son, Ashley. This dissatisfaction with his work, the preoccupation he seemed to have with Maddie... It was all because he hadn't had sex in eight months and that alone was enough to turn a man slightly crazy.

'The very person we're looking for.' Mrs Ralston beamed when she saw him. 'We want a picture of you holding Ashley. Now, no false modesty, Doctor,' she continued when Gabriel began to shake his head. 'We know Ashley wouldn't be going home today if it hadn't been for your skill.'

'It was a team effort, Mrs Ralston,' he insisted. 'I'm just one member of the team.'

'I'd give in gracefully if I were you, Mr Dalgleish.' Maddie chuckled. 'This is one argument you aren't going to win.'

He wouldn't, he realised, and ruefully he took Ashley from his mother's outstretched hands. 'Where do you want me to stand?'

'I just want your biggest smile,' Maddie said, putting the camera to her eye, then lowering it again with amused exasperation. 'Oh, come on, Mr Dalgleish, you can do better than that. Think of it as practice for the future if you ever become a father.'

A father? Never in his life had he thought of having children, but as Ashley kicked his legs and burbled up at him, and he watched Maddie waggling her fingers to try to get the baby's attention, he suddenly found himself thinking, Why not?

*Because you're a career consultant, you idiot,* his mind pointed out, *and kids mean nappies, and teething, and sleepless nights, not to mention the fact that you're lousy with kids. Look at how you screwed up with Charlie, and you're dead in the water with Susie.*

'Thank you so much,' Mr Ralston said when Maddie gave him back his camera. 'Now I'd like one of you with Ashley.'

'Me?' she protested. 'But I'm just a secretary.'

'No, you're not,' Mrs Ralston insisted. 'You've listened to our worries, provided a shoulder for us to cry on, cheered us up when we were down, so we want a photograph of you, too.'

'Oh, come on, Maddie,' Gabriel said, grinning wickedly at her. 'Think of it as practice for the future if you ever become a mother.'

'Not on your life,' she muttered under her breath, and he laughed, but when she took Ashley from him, and cradled him against her breast, he lost his breath.

She might say she didn't want to be a mother but with Ashley in her arms she looked like the kind of mother he would have killed for when he'd been a child. The kind of mother who would turn up every school sports day to cheer her kids on, whether they came first or last. The kind of mother who would break out the triple chocolate ice cream to congratulate or commiserate, whereas he…

If he could have taken a degree in raising kids he would probably have passed the theory with honours, but when it came to the practical he'd undoubtedly have got a big, fat zero and that hurt a lot more than he could ever have imagined it would.

'You look like a man whose just lost a pound and found a penny,' Maddie said, gazing up at him curiously after the Ralstons had gone. 'What's wrong?'

He was damned if he knew. Before today he'd never once thought of having children, so why was he getting himself in such a lather about something that might never happen?

'Are Susie and Charlie all set for tomorrow?' he asked, deliberately changing the subject, and she smiled ruefully.

'Would you believe Charlie wants to take his football with him? I've told him absolutely not. Not with all those windows at Pollok House.'

He laughed. 'And Susie?'

'She's looking forward to it, too,' she replied, but he knew from the way she wasn't meeting his gaze that she was lying.

Susie was the rock on which he could stumble, the fly in his ointment. He'd known it last Saturday, and he'd hoped the girl might have mellowed since then, but she clearly hadn't. *Got to be extra pleasant to Susie tomorrow.*

'What about you?' he said. 'Are you looking forward to our day out?'

'Very much,' she said, and as she smiled up at him his heart picked up speed.

Damn, but he wanted her. Wanted to touch the lush soft curve of her breast, wanted to taste her full lips, and all he had to do was get through tomorrow. If he could get through tomorrow without upsetting either Charlie or Susie, he would be home and dry. It shouldn't be difficult. Charlie had already forgiven him and as for Susie… She was just a kid—albeit a truculent one—and if he was extra-pleasant to her tomorrow how could he possibly fail?

Maddie walked down the gravel path into the gardens surrounding Pollok House and vowed that if Gabriel hadn't throttled Susie by the end of the day, she was going to.

From the minute they'd arrived at Pollok House, Gabriel had tried to interest her niece in the beautiful paintings and china on display, had listened uncomplainingly to Charlie's constant chatter, treated them all to lunch in the Edwardian restaurant, and yet Susie had done nothing but trail moodily behind them, making snarky comments. *If Susie had been four instead of fourteen, she'd have been going straight home to bed,* Maddie decided.

'Which part of the house did you like best, Charlie?' she asked, knowing that he, at least, could be guaranteed to be enthusiastic.

'Everything.' He beamed as he skipped ahead of them on the path. 'But my most favourite was seeing all those people dressed up as servants and members of the family.'

'I think that's a dumb idea,' Susie declared. 'Dressing up in old clothes doesn't give you any idea of what it must have been like to have lived in another century.'

'True,' Gabriel said evenly. 'But a lot of visitors like it and it probably brings in much-needed money for the house's upkeep.'

'It's still dumb,' Susie said caustically, and Maddie gritted her teeth until they hurt.

'I liked the dinner sets,' she said determinedly. 'And the El Greco painting—*The Lady in the Fur Wrap*—was absolutely stunning.'

'That was my favourite, too,' Gabriel observed. 'What did you think of it, Susie?'

'Personally—*personally*—I think it's obscene for any one family to own so much,' Susie said defiantly, and Gabriel smiled at her.

'I couldn't agree more, but when I visit houses like this it's to admire the skill and craftsmanship of the men and women who created all the beautiful things, not to envy the owners.'

*And that's taken the wind well and truly out of your sails, Susie,* Maddie thought, biting back a chuckle as she saw her niece scowl.

'Gabe, what's that river called?' Charlie asked, pointing to the meandering stream ahead of him.

'The White Cart and, before you ask me why, I don't have the faintest idea,' Gabriel said, shooting Maddie a smile.

A smile she felt all the way down to her toes. A smile which had her wishing—not for the first time that day—that she hadn't insisted on Charlie and Susie accompanying them.

Except that going anywhere alone with Gabriel was a recipe for disaster. She'd already spent far too much time today scoping out his lips, and wondering if they'd feel warm and gentle like Jonah's, or hot and demanding as they always were in her dreams, and that was with Charlie and Susie acting as chaperones. If she'd been alone with him…

Oh, hell, if she'd been alone with him she would have thrown all caution to the wind. She would have been more than willing to let him wrap his arms around her, let him kiss her, let him press his hard length against her. She closed her eyes briefly to enjoy the image, only to realise when she reopened them that Gabriel was watching her.

'Penny for them, Maddie?' he said, his voice deep, husky, and she shook her head.

'Not worth it, Gabriel,' she said, and he smiled again, a knowing smile that brought hot colour flooding into her cheeks.

'I'm fed up with walking,' Susie said, her small face mutinous. 'Can't we sit down for a rest?'

'How about sitting down here on the grass?' Gabriel suggested. 'It's bone dry—and Charlie won't come to any harm, Maddie,' he continued, seeing her glance uncertainly to where Charlie was throwing stones into the river. 'The water's very shallow.'

'OK, then,' she said, sitting down on the grass, but as Gabriel sat down beside her he tilted his head slightly and grinned.

'You're getting freckles.'

'I always do if I don't wear sunscreen,' she said, rubbing her nose self-consciously. 'I did bring some with me, but I left it in the glove compartment of your car.'

He dug his car keys out of his pocket. 'Susie, could you go and get your aunt's sunscreen, please?'

That Susie didn't want to go was clear, but she took the keys from him with singularly bad grace then stomped off up the gravel path. Maddie sighed.

'I'm sorry she's been such a pain in the butt today.'

'Has she?' Gabriel smiled, and she laughed.

'Nice try, but no sale. If I'd been in your shoes I think I would have slapped her.'

'No, you wouldn't,' he said. 'In fact, I doubt if you ever get really angry with either Charlie or Susie.'

She shook her head ruefully. 'You couldn't be more wrong.'

'But—'

'Gabriel, please, don't run away with the idea that I'm some sort of super-aunt,' she said. 'There are days when the children hate me, days when I dislike them intensely.' *Today being one of those days in Susie's case.* 'I lose my temper with them, get myself trapped into corners before I've even seen the corner coming. Everybody who looks after children does.'

'But you seem to understand them so well,' he said, bewilderment plain on his face. 'Be able to relate to them so easily. How did you learn to do that?'

'If I'm getting anything right it's because I've tried to copy the way my mum and dad brought me up. If I stepped out of line they told me off. If I was unhappy or achieved something—no matter how small—they gave me masses of hugs and kisses, and if they were wrong they always apologised.'

'If I were to bring up children the way I was brought up they'd all be in therapy by the time they were ten,' he murmured, and he looked so unhappy that she instinctively reached out and laced her fingers with his.

'Jonah told me a little bit about your childhood,' she said gently. 'How…how difficult it was for you.'

'Difficult?' he said savagely. 'Oh, yes, I guess you could call it difficult.'

He was clearly remembering the past, and she knew she should leave it there, but she had to ask, she just had to.

'Gabriel, why—given your background—did you say what you said to Charlie about his grades?' she asked.

At first she didn't think he was going to answer, and when he finally spoke his voice was tight, constricted.

'I think…I think it was because I was so totally thrown by your kids.'

'They're not that bad, are they?' she teased, trying to lighten his mood, but it didn't work.

'I'm not used to meeting children who can talk, Maddie, and Susie… She kept looking at me, clearly thinking, *Who is this idiot?* And Charlie was completely ignoring me. I'm not used to feeling uncomfortable, I'm used to being in control, so I just said the first thing that came into my head.' He shook his head. 'Unfortunately it was what my bloody parents always used to say to me.'

'But why—?'

'Why didn't I take it back immediately?' he interrupted. 'I

didn't know how to. We Dalgleishes…' His mouth twisted into a bitter parody of a smile. 'We Dalgleishes don't make mistakes, you see.'

'Omnipotent are you?' She smiled, hoping for a proper smile from him but it didn't come.

'Something like that.'

'Gabriel, it isn't wrong or a sign of failure to make a mistake and then admit you've made it,' she said, and he sighed.

'It was in my home. In my home you were a success, or you were nothing, less than nothing.'

She was appalled. How could anybody treat a child like that? How could any parent withhold or grant love on the basis of success or failure? Her heart went out to him for the childhood he'd never had, the love and comfort he'd never received when he'd been a boy.

'Oh, Gabriel, I'm sorry—so sorry,' she said, through a throat so tight it hurt. 'I wish I could make it right for you—wipe out the memories you have—'

'You do,' he interrupted, and, before she realised what was he was going to do, he'd raised her hand to his lips. 'You do, Maddie, just by being you.'

His voice was soft and gentle and she felt her heart twist and clench inside her with a pain that was so real she almost gasped out loud. *Don't do this to me,* she thought. *Don't do this if you don't mean it, because I think I'm falling in love with you, and if I fall in love with you, and you walk away from me, as Andrew and Colin did, I don't think I'll be able to bear it.*

'Gabriel…' There was heat in his eyes, but she could see confusion and bewilderment there, too, as though he didn't quite know what was happening either. 'I think—'

'Here's your sunscreen, Aunt Maddie,' Susie interrupted, thrusting the tube at her, then flopping belligerently down between her and Gabriel. 'How much longer are we going to have to stay in this dump? I'm bored.'

'We'll be going home soon, Susie,' Gabriel said, and Maddie drew in a shuddering breath.

She didn't want to go home. At least here—out in the open with the kids—she couldn't do anything stupid, but at home… At home she'd make them all tea, and then they'd probably watch some TV, but not even she could insist that the children stay up until Gabriel had left. Eventually, both Charlie and Susie would go to bed, and then she and Gabriel would be alone, and what was she going to do then?

Half past eleven, Maddie thought with relief as she watched Susie trudge reluctantly up the stairs to her bedroom. Charlie had gone to bed a little before nine, completely tired out from his day at Pollok House, but Susie had hung about downstairs, finding a hundred and one things she absolutely had to do.

*Thank you, Susie.*

Which was wrong, and cowardly, but right now she felt cowardly. Right now her emotions were far too confused for her to be able to think straight, and all she wanted was for Gabriel to leave.

'She doesn't like me very much, does she?' Gabriel said when Maddie went back into the sitting room.

She wished she could deny it, but she couldn't. Even if she had been the most rose-tinted aunt in the world she couldn't have denied that Susie had been thoroughly obnoxious all day.

'Charlie likes you,' she replied, deliberately sidestepping his question, but it didn't work.

'Charlie's easy to like, but Susie…' He shook his head ruefully. 'She's a whole different ball game.'

'She's a teenager,' she said. 'Being stroppy comes with the territory.'

'I guess so,' he said, and Maddie bit her lip.

'I'm sorry you had such a rotten time today.'

'I didn't.' He smiled. 'In fact, I'd very much like to go out with you again.'

'You would?' she said faintly. 'But I thought you meant…'

'That Susie's behaviour had put me off?' He shook his head. 'Water off a duck's back.'

She chuckled a little uncertainly. 'You must be either a saint or a masochist to want to go out with Susie and Charlie again.'

She saw the dismay in his dark grey eyes as he registered that she was suggesting yet another family date, and her heart whispered, *Let him off the hook. Get a sitter in to look after Charlie and Susie next Saturday and go out with him alone.*

But she couldn't let him off the hook, she knew she couldn't. She had to take this slowly. For her sake, for Susie and Charlie's sake, she had to be certain.

'How about we take them to the Burrell Collection next Saturday?' she suggested, and he stood up.

'Sounds good to me. And now I'd better be going.'

'You're leaving?' she said. *Oh, hell, Maddie, be consistent here. First you let Susie stay up to all hours so you don't have to be alone with him, and now he's going, you want him to stay.*

'It's late, and I have to work tomorrow,' he reminded her.

Of course he did. He normally worked 24/7 so for him to have taken a day off at all was absolutely amazing.

'I had a lovely time at Pollok House,' she said as she walked with him to her front door, 'and I know Charlie did, too. As for Susie… All I can say is your tolerance was above and beyond the call of duty.'

He laughed, but when she reached out to open the front door he put his hand over hers to stay her.

'Maddie…'

He was going to kiss her. She knew without a shadow of a doubt that he was going to kiss her, and of course he was. Jonah had kissed her at the end of their date, so Gabriel was bound to want to kiss her, too, and she wanted him to kiss her, but what if his kiss didn't turn out any better than Jonah's had? What if the simple truth was that she was a lousy kisser? It would be so humiliating.

*Don't panic,* she told herself as he put his arms around her. *You can do this. You just close your eyes and pucker up. Oh, and you relax,* she reminded herself as he drew her closer and she felt herself stiffen. *You relax and you tilt your head. But not that far back. You're tilting it way too far back!* Quickly she tried to move her head round and—

'Oh! Ouch—ouch!' she gasped, hearing his sharp intake of breath and feeling her own eyes water as the side of his head banged into her nose. 'I'm sorry—so sorry. Are you all right?'

'Are *you* all right?' he said quickly, concern on his face. 'Your nose—it's not broken, is it?'

*Oh, please, God, don't let my nose be broken,* she thought, putting her fingers to it quickly. She would just die of mortification if their date ended with her in A and E with a broken nose.

'It's OK—I'm sure it's OK,' she said. 'Are you OK?'

'Well, apart from a strange ringing in my ears, and all those stars I keep seeing… Joke, Maddie, *joke.*' He grinned as she gazed at him in horror. 'I'm fine, honestly I am, so let's try that again. But this time,' he added, reaching out and cupping her face firmly in his hands, 'this time we'll try it this way.'

*Smart move,* she thought. *Keep my head trapped so I can't do you any more damage. OK, Maddie, you can do this,* she told herself as his lips came down towards hers again. *Just relax, and don't screw it up again.*

And she didn't screw it up. The moment his lips met hers she didn't have to think about relaxing, or getting it wrong, because his lips fitted hers so perfectly. Fitted them with a heat that made her tremble. Fitted them with a warmth that made her so dizzy she had to clutch at his shirt to steady herself, and before she could rationalise what she was doing she was kissing him back, tasting the heat of him, feeling her own blood surge, wanting him closer, closer. Suddenly he jerked away from her, breathing hard, leaving her giddy and confused, until she heard what he had—an angry voice exclaiming, '*Aunt Maddie.*'

'Susie…?' Maddie said breathlessly, glancing over her shoulder to see her niece standing in her dressing-gown at the foot of the stairs, her eyes stormy. 'I… Is there something wrong?'

'Charlie's very restless. I thought you should know.' She scowled at Gabriel. 'I thought you'd gone.'

'I'm sorry, Gabriel,' Maddie said, regret plain on her face. 'Charlie still has the occasional nightmare so I have to go to him, settle him down.'

'Is there anything I can do to help?' he asked.

*Yes, stay here, wait here, and when I come back make love to me,* she thought, but that was a bad idea, and she knew it was.

'Not really,' she said. 'Thank you for a lovely day, and I'm looking forward to next week.'

'My pleasure,' he said, and he leant towards her, and she leant forward, too, hoping he might kiss her again.

Susie said, 'Aunt Maddie, Charlie *really* needs you.' Reluctantly Maddie stepped back.

'Goodnight, then,' she said.

'Sweet dreams.' Gabriel smiled, and Maddie threw him a smile as she hurried up the stairs. He was left with Susie who was gazing at him with no warmth at all.

Well, he didn't like her very much at the moment either, he thought grimly.

'Next week?' Susie demanded, and it took him a few seconds to work out what she was talking about.

'Your aunt and I are taking you and Charlie to the Burrell Collection next week.'

'So I have to put up with yet another let's-all-play-happy-families date, do I?' Susie said, not even trying to hide her contempt.

'It's late, Susie,' he said tightly. 'If you'll excuse me—'

'You're going to break my Aunt Maddie's heart, aren't you?' Susie said as he opened the door, and he swung round to her, open-mouthed.

'I'm going to *what?*' he said.

'I love her, and I don't want her to be unhappy, but you...' A half-sob broke from her. 'You're going to break her heart.'

'Susie, listen to me—'

'No, *you* listen,' she cried. 'My Aunt Maddie...she's special. She doesn't deserve to be mucked about, so if you're not going to be here for the duration, if all you want is to get her into your bed and then leave, please, just go away now and never come back.'

Gabriel thrust his fingers through his hair, and tried to marshal his thoughts. Hell, the girl was talking happy ever afters, and he was still struggling to dampen down his libido and get his reeling head back in gear.

'Susie, I like your aunt very much,' he began. 'I like being with her, talking to her, and I'm attracted to her—I can't deny that—but whether we have a future together... All we can do is spend time together, and see what happens.'

'That isn't an answer,' she protested. 'That's all woolly maybes and could bes, and I want to *know.*'

Lord, but she suddenly looked so very young staring back at him, her brown eyes confused and unhappy, and he wished he could give her a definite answer, but he couldn't because he didn't know the answer himself.

He knew that when Maddie smiled up at him his heart beat faster. He knew that when she was close to him he longed to reach out and make love to her, but as for him making a long-term commitment to her, and to her children... That was something else entirely. That was way beyond anything he'd experienced in the past, and he wasn't ready to deal with it now.

'Susie, I have to go,' he said.

'But—'

'It's late, Susie,' he said, and before she could say anything else he strode out of the door and down to his car, knowing she watched him the whole way.

# CHAPTER EIGHT

GABRIEL leant back in his seat and gazed morosely out of his consulting-room window at the buildings across the street and the blue sky beyond.

Four stricken Saturdays. Four let's-play-happy-families Saturdays, and the only physical contact he'd had with Maddie had been two stolen kisses, both interrupted by Susie. If he didn't have Maddie soon he was going to go crazy.

'Diana's latest blood test results are back,' Jonah said as he strode into the consulting room. 'I'm afraid your suspicions were correct. She does have another infection.'

'Right,' Gabriel replied, without turning round.

'I've told Lynne to increase the antibiotics she's already on, and to monitor her heart rate in case the stronger dosage interferes with her heart medication.'

'Fine.'

'I've also told Lynne that while this heat wave lasts I'd like all of the babies to wear bikinis.'

'OK,' Gabriel said, then looked round sharply. 'What did you just say?'

'I thought you weren't listening.' Jonah laughed as he put the folder he was holding down on Gabriel's desk, but when Gabriel didn't join in his laughter he stared at him thoughtfully for a moment, then pulled over a chair and sat down. 'OK, what's up?'

'Just Monday morning blues,' Gabriel replied, but Jonah shook his head.

'Gabriel, you've been walking around the unit strung tighter than a wire for the past two weeks, so why don't you just tell me what's wrong before you blow a fuse?'

'It's personal,' Gabriel said tightly, and Jonah folded his arms and sat further back in his seat.

'OK, I'm good with personal, and if this has anything to do with Maddie—and I suspect it has—you know I don't gossip, so what's wrong?'

Gabriel hesitated for a second, then a month's worth of frustration spilled out.

'It's her kids, Jonah. Maddie and I have been out on four dates, and every time her kids have come with us. I know she said I had to get to know them but, damn it, we're never alone. In the past four weeks I've taken them to Pollok House, the Burrell Collection, the People's Palace, the Museum of Transport—'

'All that culture and all you want to do is get laid.' Jonah grinned.

'No, I don't,' Gabriel protested, then coloured slightly when Jonah's eyebrows rose. 'OK, maybe I do, but—'

'Gabriel, if you just wanted sex with no strings attached, you shouldn't be dating a woman like Maddie.'

'I don't just want sex,' Gabriel declared, 'but, hell's bells, Jonah, we haven't even been able to kiss properly without Susie popping up like some junior member of the vice squad.'

Jonah smothered a laugh. 'She sounds just like my kid sister. I remember once when I was in high school—'

'Jonah…'

'OK, OK.' Jonah grinned. 'You don't want to hear about my past, but has it ever occurred to you that maybe Maddie *wants* these interruptions?'

'Why in the world would she want them?' Gabriel demanded, and Jonah shook his head at him.

'Think about it, Gabriel. Dating somebody new is tough enough at the best of times but when you have kids you're not just putting yourself on the line, you're putting them on the line with you. I think these family dates are Maddie's way of protecting them because the last thing she wants is Charlie and Susie getting fond of you and then you take off, dumping them as well as her.'

'Which means more of these damn happy family jaunts.' Gabriel sighed. Jonah nodded. 'I'm afraid so. How are you actually getting on with Charlie and Susie?'

'Charlie…' Unconsciously Gabriel's face softened. 'He just wants somebody to listen to him. Maddie does really well, but she's not a guy so she doesn't always understand his worries. I've been trying to give him as much help and advice as I can, but it's difficult when I only see him once a week.'

'You're giving him advice?' Jonah said with surprise, and Gabriel shrugged.

'It's the least I can do, and he…well, he seems to sort of look up to me, for some reason.'

'Interesting,' Jonah said. 'And Susie?'

Gabriel grimaced. 'She hates my guts.'

'Nah, she doesn't. She just loves her aunt, and you're this interloper who might be on the level and then again might not. If you let her see you're one of the good guys, she'll come round.'

Yeah, when hell freezes over, Gabriel thought gloomily.

'And Maddie?' Jonah said. 'Apart from the no-sex thing, are you enjoying spending time with her?'

He was. He couldn't remember ever having laughed as much with a woman as he had with Maddie, but he was a man, not a monk, and being in her company, yet not being able to make love to her, was pushing his self-restraint to the limit. And this hot weather wasn't helping. The entire female staff of the Belfield seemed to have jettisoned their pantyhose, but it was Maddie's bare legs his eyes kept straying towards, Maddie's short T-shirts his eyes drifted to every time she stretched up, because he knew he would catch a tantalising glimpse of bare midriff.

Which was pathetic. A man of his age shouldn't be reduced to sneaking glances at a woman's bare legs and midriff, but he was so darned frustrated he'd have accepted a glimpse of a bare anything.

'If I were in your shoes I'd be cheering that nobody at the Belfield has sussed out yet that the two of you are dating,' Jonah continued, clearly oblivious to his thoughts. 'I don't know how you're getting away with it, but at the moment only Nell and I know and we won't talk.'

There wasn't anything for them to talk about anyway, Gabriel thought sourly, but he didn't say that.

'I'd be grateful if you could keep it under your hat for as long as you can,' he said instead.

'So, you're in this with Maddie for the duration, are you?' Jonah said, and Gabriel only just restrained himself from saying something unprintable.

Hell's bells, first Susie and now Jonah. He couldn't promise a happy-ever-after ending. Nobody could. Maybe after he'd made love to Maddie he might know if they were heading for a long-term relationship, but until then it was like asking a man if he was going to keep on buying a particular brand of biscuits when he hadn't even tasted them.

'Those blood results for Diana,' Gabriel said, deliberately changing the subject. 'She definitely has another infection?'

Jonah gave him a hard stare that told him he knew exactly what he was doing. 'Yes, but about Maddie—'

'She's certainly getting her unfair share of them,' Gabriel continued determinedly, 'but, then, Ben Thompson did, too, and I'd say he only needs another couple of days in Special Care and we can transfer him to Transitional.'

Jonah gave up. 'Agreed. So, are you ready for your morning rounds?'

Gabriel wasn't. He was hot, he had the beginnings of a headache, and it was only Monday morning, which meant he had another five days to get through before he went out with Maddie again. Or more precisely, went out with Maddie, Charlie and Susie again. He sighed at the thought. Other men took their dates out to the movies on a Saturday, or to a restaurant for a meal, and then, if they got lucky, it was back to their flats for some fun—but what did he get? Culture with Charlie and Susie.

'Gabriel?'

Jonah was waiting for him, and he knew if he told him what he was thinking he'd get another lecture on how important it was for him to take things slowly. And he *would* take things slowly, he told himself as he followed Jonah out into the corridor, but whoever said suffering was good for the soul had clearly never dated Maddie Bryce.

'That's the last time I believe the weather forecast,' Nell said as she sipped a lime soda in Maddie's office and wafted a makeshift paper fan in front of her face in a vain attempt to create a little breeze. 'Slightly cooler on Wednesday, they said. Well, unless this heat has addled my brains, this is Wednesday and I think it's even hotter today.'

'I never thought I'd hear myself say this,' Maddie said, easing her damp T-shirt back from the nape of her neck, 'but it can be too hot. It's fine if you can spend your time lazing on a beach, but when you have to work…'

'Speaking of lazing about,' Nell said, 'where are you and Gabriel taking the kids this Saturday?'

'I thought we might go to the Science Centre.'

'Oh, hell, Maddie, why don't you give the poor bloke a break?' Nell laughed. 'Not only is it hot enough to fry an egg on the pavement out there, but in the past four weeks he's taken you to Pollok House, the People's Palace, the—'

'He enjoyed it—or at least he said he did,' Maddie protested. 'And since when did you care where we went anyway? You don't think I should be dating him at all.'

'I've changed my mind. Any bloke who's prepared to put up with Susie and Charlie, plus mega-doses of culture every Saturday, must be on the level.'

'You reckon?' Maddie said, despising herself for needing confirmation but wanting it anyway.

'Don't you?' Nell said in surprise. 'I mean, I assumed—as you're still dating—that the two of you were getting on like a house on fire both in the going-out-as-a-family stakes and in the bed department.'

Maddie took a sip of her own lime soda, then cleared her throat uncomfortably. 'There isn't any bed department.'

Nell's eyes widened. 'You're kidding. Gabriel and you haven't made love yet?'

'When would we have had the opportunity?' Maddie said defensively. 'We spend every Saturday with the kids, and when we get home Susie doesn't go to bed until late.'

Nell put down her makeshift fan. 'Maddie, if Susie's up late it's because you *want* her to stay up late.'

'No, I don't. OK, maybe I do,' she admitted as Nell's eyebrows rose, 'but I'm just not comfortable about the idea of making love to Gabriel when the kids are in the house. What if Charlie had a nightmare and came looking for me, or Susie got up for a glass of water and walked in on us?'

'Copout,' Nell said firmly. 'If you really wanted to make love to him, you know I'd let the kids stay overnight with me, so what's the real reason behind these no-sex dates?'

Maddie bit her lip. 'I'm scared, Nell. I like him—I like him a lot. When he's near me, when he smiles at me...all I want to do is jump on him and say, "Make love to me," but it's such a big gamble, such a big risk. You know what my track record in men is like. I pick stinkers. Time and time again, I pick stinkers.'

'You think Gabriel is a stinker?'

Maddie thought about it. Then she thought about it some more. 'I don't know, Nell. I don't think he is, but I don't know, not for certain.'

'Want to hear some stop-press news, Maddie? There are no certainties when it comes to relationships. All you can do is trust your instincts.'

'And if my instincts are wrong?' Maddie said.

'Then you live with it like the rest of us do,' Nell said. 'But you're going to have to come to some decision about him soon because it seems to me as though he's meeting all of your conditions and you're giving him nothing in return.'

'He likes spending time with Charlie,' Maddie said defensively, and Nell sighed.

'I'm sure he does, but this isn't about Charlie and Susie, is it, Maddie? It's about you.'

No, it wasn't, Maddie thought. It could never be solely about her, and there was another thing Nell hadn't considered, but she had. If she gave in to her fear and told Gabriel that all she wanted from him was friendship, he probably wouldn't want to spend time with her any more, and she'd miss him. She'd miss him very much.

'Lynne only has another two months to go before she leaves for New Zealand,' she said, deliberately changing the subject. 'Are you going to apply for her job?'

Nell shot her a look that said, *I haven't finished talking about Gabriel yet, so don't think you're off the hook.*

'I don't know,' she said. 'Part of me says, "Go for it," but the other part thinks, "Yikes, it's an awful lot of extra responsibility."'

'You can do it,' Maddie insisted. 'You've got both the knowledge and the experience.'

'You reckon?'

'Of course I do,' Maddie insisted. 'Look, will you at least think about it?'

A small smile curved Nell's lips. 'OK, I'll make a deal with you,' her cousin said. 'I'll think about applying for Lynne's job if you promise to make up your mind about Gabriel.'

'Nell…'

'Is it a deal?' Nell put out her hand and, after a second's hesitation, Maddie took it.

'OK, it's a deal,' she said. But all she was going to do was think about it, and if that was cowardly, then she was cowardly.

On Friday Gabriel didn't think his week could get any tougher, but it did. Maternity had four premature births and, with no babies in the unit anywhere near stable enough to be transferred to Special Care, he spent a frustrating morning phoning around every NICU in the country to see if any of them could take them.

'This is ridiculous, Jonah!' he exclaimed as he swept down the corridor. 'We shouldn't have to be sending babies hundreds of miles away from their mothers.'

'I agree,' Jonah replied, 'but the likelihood of us ever getting a bigger unit is nil. The funding just isn't available.'

'Then it should be,' Gabriel snapped. 'Every baby has the right to the best possible care and it should never depend upon whether we've got an empty incubator available.'

'I agree. And speaking of babies getting the best possible care, the Scotts look a lot happier today,' Jonah said, motioning to where the couple were standing outside Gabriel's consulting room.

They were.

'Diana's a real fighter, isn't she, Mr Dalgleish?' Simon said, his voice a mixture of relief and pride as Gabriel ushered him and his wife into his consulting room. 'That's another infection she's managed to throw off. It doesn't seem to matter what life throws at her, she just keeps on battling.'

'She does indeed,' Gabriel replied. 'Did Sister Howard tell you we'll be giving her another blood transfusion this afternoon?'

'She's had a lot of those, hasn't she?' Rhona said, and Gabriel nodded, then paused.

Was a simple nod enough, or did Mrs Scott's comment imply a deeper fear? Hell, but ever since Maddie had told him about the importance of listening to people he felt as though he spent half his working day trying to second-guess what anybody said to him. OK, he'd assume Rhona's comment wasn't simply a generalised observation, and hope he was right.

'I know she seems to be having rather a lot of blood transfusions,' he said, 'but the problem is we need to take blood from her for testing to make sure she isn't developing a condition we're unaware of, and in a child as small as Diana even a teaspoon of her blood is too much for her to lose.'

'Oh, I see,' Rhona said, and smiled across at her husband, who smiled back. 'That makes perfect sense.'

Maybe he was finally getting the hang of this listening business, Gabriel thought with relief.

'I can't believe Diana is almost six weeks old,' Simon Scott observed. 'It seems no time at all since she was born, and she's doing so well, isn't she? The ventricular tapping thing is working, her heart problem seems to be resolving by itself, and though she's had a lot of infections she's come through them all.'

Gabriel nodded. The resilience of tiny babies never ceased to amaze him, and though Diana still had a long way to go, even he was beginning to feel cautiously optimistic.

'She's doing remarkably well,' he said.

*He* wasn't, he realised when the couple left to visit their daughter. The week had seemed interminable and the one thing that had kept him going was the thought of Saturday, but how many more of these family Saturdays would Maddie insist on—how many more would he be able to stand? Sure, he enjoyed talking to Charlie, but he hadn't asked Maddie out in order to spend his time socialising with her nephew.

Maybe he should give Maddie an ultimatum, tell her that unless he could go out with her properly he didn't want to see her again. Evelyn had made it clear she was available and at least with her he wouldn't be so frustrated all the time. Except Evelyn didn't make him laugh the way Maddie did, and her smile didn't make his heart quicken the way Maddie's did.

'You're in a bad way, Gabriel,' he muttered as he left his consulting room, and heard a soft laugh behind him.

'First signs. Talking to yourself.'

He glanced over his shoulder to see Maddie smiling at him.

'Only if you answer yourself back,' he replied. 'Were you looking for me?'

'I was, and I'm afraid I have some disappointing news,' she said, regret plain in her face. 'Charlie and Susie's grandparents phoned last night to say they'd like to see them so I'm driving them through to Edinburgh tomorrow, which means our day out will have to be cancelled.'

'I'm surprised they still remember they have grandchildren,' he said, disappointment roughening his voice. 'Isn't it four months since they last saw them?'

'Helen and Bill are in their seventies, Gabriel, and they don't have a car. Trips through to Glasgow aren't easy for them.'

'No, but dumping Charlie and Susie on you clearly is,' he said, and her face set slightly.

'They didn't *dump* them on me,' she said, with an edge. 'I volunteered to take them because they couldn't cope. You know how difficult Susie can be, and Charlie—'

'There's nothing wrong with Charlie,' he flared, and her face relaxed slightly.

'Not when he's with you, there's not. Look, if you still want to see the children, we should be back from Edinburgh by six. If you come round at seven we could take the kids to the cinema.'

But he didn't want to sit in the dark for a couple of hours, watching some kids' movie. He wanted to hold her, to kiss her, to make love to her.

'Or perhaps you'd rather just forget Saturday completely?' she said, sensing his reluctance.

Part of him wanted to say forget it, but that would mean he'd have to wait yet another week before he could go out with her and if they went to the cinema he could at least hold hands with her, under the cover of darkness without Susie popping up and doing her chastity patrol bit.

*Oh, for crying out loud, Gabriel. Holding hands in the dark? You really do need to get a proper love life.*

'Gabriel...?'

'I'll come round at seven,' he said.

This wasn't how Saturday was supposed to end, Maddie thought as she sat nervously in her kitchen, watching the clock on the wall tick relentlessly towards seven o'clock. Charlie and Susie were supposed to spend the day with their grandparents, and then Gabriel would take them all out to the cinema in the evening. But now...

'You're sure you don't mind the children staying overnight with us?' Bill had said. 'It's just that we've so enjoyed their company. I'm sorry we don't have a spare bed for you, but...'

'And I'm sure Maddie would much rather enjoy a little time to herself.' Helen had smiled, and Maddie had tried to smile back, but all she'd been able to think was that Gabriel was coming round tonight, and if the children weren't there she was going to be all alone with him.

It's just a date, she'd tried to tell herself as she'd driven back to Glasgow. People go out on dates all the time. It's no big deal.

But she knew that it was. For the past four weeks she'd insisted on never seeing Gabriel alone, and now Gabriel was going to arrive, expecting to see Charlie and Susie, and when she told him they weren't there he was bound to think she was saying, *I'm available.*

*Well, you are, aren't you?* a little voice whispered in her head. *Look at what you're wearing. Your powder blue sundress, the one that buttons all the way down the front, the one you don't need to wear a bra with. If that's not saying* I'm available, *I don't know what is.*

Oh, hell, maybe she should change into something else, even though her sundress was the coolest thing she possessed. Maybe she could pretend to be out when he called. Or maybe, she decided as her front doorbell rang and she walked slowly down the hall to answer it, she should just grow up, stop agonising, and relax.

And then again, perhaps not, she thought when she opened the door.

Lord, but he suddenly looked so big. Big, and masculine, and downright sexy, and she could feel her heart doing an involved tango that had nothing to do with the heat.

'Is something wrong?' he said with a slight frown. 'You look a little stressed.'

'Do I?' she said, annoyingly aware that her voice had come out way too high. *Get a grip, Maddie. Nothing is going to happen here tonight that you don't want to happen.* 'It's probably the heat. I'm not good in the heat.'

'Neither am I,' he said, pulling his shirt away from the back of his neck as she led the way into the sitting room. 'So, which movie do the kids want to see tonight?'

She sucked in a lungful of air. This was it. Crunch time.

'They're not here,' she said, feeling her cheeks beginning to darken with every word. 'Their grandparents asked if they could stay with them tonight.'

His eyes met hers, and she saw the surprise in them give way to something darker that sent her already skittering heart into overdrive.

'So it's just us this evening,' he said.

She nodded. Just us, in an empty house, with nobody to interrupt us. Just us. All alone.

'So, what would you like to do?' he said. 'Take in a movie, go out to dinner or, if you're too tired after your visit to Edinburgh, would you prefer to get in a take-away and watch some TV?'

*I want you to make love to me. No, I don't. Yes, I do. Nell said I had to come to a decision, and I have. I want you to make love to me.*

'Maddie…?'

He was staring at her curiously—probably thinking, *Dear Lord, I'm dating a complete flake,* she thought—and she pasted a smile to her lips.

'I think I'd rather stay home,' she said. 'I have some chicken and salad in the fridge. Charlie and Susie don't like either but I do.'

'Perfect.' He smiled, that lopsided, slightly crooked smile that always did strange things to her brain, and she shook her head to clear it.

Food. He wanted food. The food was in the kitchen. If he stayed in the sitting room maybe she'd be able to get her act together.

And she did. She managed to prepare the chicken salad, and they ate it and drank some of the bottle of wine she found lurking in the fridge, and he switched on the TV, and by the time she'd sat through two game shows and a comedy that wasn't even remotely funny her nerves were stretched to breaking point.

Every time he moved her heart clenched. Every time their eyes met she had difficulty breathing. She wanted him. She wanted him so much, but for some strange reason his gaze kept drifting across to the photographs of Charlie and Susie on the mantelpiece, and the more he looked at them, the grimmer his expression became.

Something was wrong. She'd expected him, if not to immediately jump on her, to at least have made some move. Hell, he'd shot her enough hot looks in the past to melt the polar ice cap and yet now, when they were alone, he hadn't even attempted to put his arm around her as they sat, side by side, on the sofa.

'Gabriel…'

'Do you want some more wine?' he asked, half rising to his feet, and she could have screamed with frustration.

'No, I don't want any more wine,' she said. 'I want… I want…'

*You. Then do something,* her heart urged, and before she could think about it, talk herself out of it, she pulled him back down onto the sofa and kissed him.

For one awful second she thought perhaps she'd read him all wrong, that he didn't want this as much as she did, and then suddenly he was kissing her back, kissing her hard, and her mouth fitted his perfectly as it always did, and she felt his tongue against hers, hot and devastating, so that when he broke the kiss she clung to him, dizzy and breathless.

'Don't stop,' she said, breathing hard into his chest. 'Don't stop.'

And he kissed her again, and she let herself fall into him, no reservations, no fear, shivering with anticipation as his hands slid up her sides, feeling a hot rush as his fingers unbuttoned her sundress and slid it off her shoulders, leaving her naked to her waist.

'God, but you're beautiful,' he said, his voice strained as he stared down at her.

'I'm too fat,' she said, moving instinctively to cover herself, torn between embarrassment and wanting him. He stayed her hands with his own. 'You're perfect,' he said simply, and she believed him, wanted him more than she'd ever wanted any man in her whole life, so that when he cupped one of her breasts and began stroking it with his thumb, she shuddered and convulsed towards him, feeling the heat spread everywhere.

*More,* she thought as he kissed her neck, then gently bit the place he'd kissed. *I want more.*

He wanted more, too. She could see it in his eyes, hear it in his ragged breathing, and he kissed her, long and deep, sending glittering sensations everywhere, behind her eyelids, in her fingertips, low inside her, and when his hand slid up under her dress, she moaned against his mouth, loving the feel of his fingers on her skin.

Then suddenly—inexplicably—he pulled back from her, breathing hard.

'What's wrong?' she said, scanning his face, as breathless as he was.

'Maddie, I'm sorry,' he said raggedly. 'I can't do this.'

'Can't do this?' she repeated. 'But I thought…I thought this was what you wanted?'

'I do.' He pulled her sundress roughly back over her shoulders and swore under his breath. 'God, help me, Maddie, I want you more than I've ever wanted any woman before, but for your sake, we have to stop.'

*'Why?'* she protested. 'I'm a fully grown, consenting adult. I know what I'm doing—'

'No, you don't,' he interrupted, 'because for you it's for ever, isn't it? And I can't give you for ever. I can't be what you want me to be, and to make love to you knowing that…' He shook his head. 'I might be a bastard, but I'm not that big a bastard.'

'You're not a bastard at all,' she said. 'You're a kind, generous, giving man.'

'Oh, Maddie, you don't know me at all,' he said grimly, and she caught hold of his hand.

'Yes, I do. You're the man who was prepared to spend an

hour and a half teaching Charlie how to kick a ball so it bounced off two trees. The man who's listened to all of Charlie's worries and made him feel good about himself. The man who's trailed Susie around more museums and big houses than I ever want to see again in my lifetime, and you did it without a word of complaint despite the fact that she was horrible to you the whole time.'

'I only did those things because I wanted to make love to you,' he muttered.

'Are you trying to tell me you don't care about Susie and Charlie at all?' she demanded. 'Because, if you are, I don't believe you.'

'Of course I care about them,' he said impatiently, 'but to be a surrogate father to them... And that's what you want, isn't it?'

'I told you I did, and you said it was all right, that you understood,' she said.

'But I didn't, not really. I...' His jaw clenched as though he didn't want to say what he was going to say, but felt he must. 'Maddie, I want to be a father. I never thought I'd hear myself say that, but I do, and I think I could cope with a baby, but to be a father to a teenager and an eight-year-old...'

'Who aren't even mine,' she said dully. 'That's what you mean, don't you?'

'No—no—it isn't that. It's...' He dragged his fingers through his hair. 'I'm all at sea with Charlie and Susie. No matter what I try, I fail.'

'You don't fail with Charlie,' she protested. 'He thinks the world of you, and as for Susie... Gabriel, bringing up children—it isn't an exam that you pass with flying colours or fail miserably. Nobody gets it right all the time. We all just stagger along, hoping we don't screw things up too badly, so stop being so hard on yourself, expecting perfection, because there's no way you're ever going to achieve it.'

'Maddie, I'm not being hard on myself, I'm being realistic,' he said. 'I can't do this. And you said that if I couldn't accept Susie and Charlie as part of the package, then I had to walk, so I'm walking now before we get in too deep.'

*But I'm already in too deep,* she thought as she stared up at him. *I've fallen in love with you so I'm already in way over my head.*

'Gabriel—'

'No, Maddie. For your sake, it has to be no.'

Nell would have said that she ought to be grateful to him for stopping when he had, that he was being sort of noble, but Maddie didn't feel grateful and she didn't think he was noble. She wanted to hit him. To hit him for all the dates they'd been out on when she'd been so sure he wanted to be with her and the children. To hit him for allowing her to believe that this time—*this time*—she'd got it right and had picked a prince instead of a frog. And she wanted to hit him most of all because, despite everything he'd said, she knew she still wanted him, and that was the worst of all.

'I think you'd better go,' she said. *Go before I totally humiliate myself and beg you to make love to me.*

'Maddie, I'm sorry.'

'You and me both,' she said tightly.

He walked slowly to the door then stopped. 'Maddie, I'd like—if I may—to see Charlie occasionally. He…he seems to sort of look up to me, and I don't want him to think I've abandoned him.'

*Like you're abandoning me?*

'I know it might be a little difficult—'

*A little?*

'But we're both mature adults. We can handle this.'

'OK,' she managed to reply, but, as she listened to him walking down the hall and then out the front door, she wanted to yell after him, *Maybe you can handle it, but I can't because what about me? What's going to happen to me?*

Tears began to trickle down her cheeks and no matter how angrily she wiped them away more kept on coming. Tears of misery and frustration. Tears that became great gulping sobs because she'd done it again. Despite all her plans and determination that this time she wouldn't screw up, she had. She'd screwed up big time.

## CHAPTER NINE

'BUT why can't we all go out with Gabe like we did before?' Charlie demanded, his small face belligerent. 'I liked going out with him. It made Saturdays special.'

'You'll still be able to see him,' Maddie said, as she had done at least twice a day since Monday, when she'd worked up the courage to tell Charlie and Susie there would be no more Saturday trips out with Gabriel. 'He said he'll come round to see you as often as he can—'

'But it won't be the *same,*' Charlie protested. 'I won't know when he's coming—I won't be able to plan.'

'Charlie—'

'This is all your fault,' he continued, rounding on his sister. 'You never stopped whining when we were out with him, and now he's had enough.'

Susie said nothing. In fact, Susie had said nothing at all about Gabriel. Not when Maddie had broken the news, or since.

'Charlie, it's nobody's fault,' Maddie insisted. 'And can you, please, get your schoolbag or you're going to be late for school.'

'It's gym on Wednesdays and I hate gym so I don't care if I'm late,' he retorted.

'Well, I care,' Maddie snapped, reaching to the end of her tether. 'If you're late, I'm late, and it's my job that pays the bills, buys us food and keeps a roof over our heads.'

'But—'

'*Enough,* Charlie,' she interrupted, and for a second he glowered defiantly back at her then whirled round and stamped out of the sitting room, slamming the door shut behind him.

'Aunt Maddie—'

'And I've heard enough from you, too, Susie,' Maddie said which was deeply unfair when her niece hadn't actually said anything, but Maddie had got beyond what was fair and what wasn't.

All she could think as she retrieved her car keys from the coffee-table was, *I don't need this. I have a headache, I haven't slept properly for days, and unless half of the population of Glasgow stays home today I'm going to be stuck in the rush hour and late for work.*

Not that Gabriel would notice. All she'd seen of him since Saturday had been the back of his head as he'd disappeared into the unit. Which was fine by her. She didn't want to talk to him either, except Nell had started frowning every time she saw her, which meant she suspected something, and Jonah had begun glancing at her curiously, too, which meant *he* was getting suspicious.

'Aunt Maddie…?'

Susie hadn't moved from where she was by the window and something in Maddie snapped.

'Are you and your brother deliberately trying to get me fired?' she demanded. 'It's half past eight, I should have dropped you both off at the pre-school activities fifteen minutes ago—'

'You liked him, didn't you?' Susie interrupted. 'You liked him a lot.'

Maddie didn't have to ask who she meant, but she didn't want to talk about Gabriel either.

'Susie, when you're older you'll realise that friendships—

relationships—between men and women don't always work out, and now can you, *please,* get ready for school?'

'It's me, isn't it?' Susie said quietly. 'If it wasn't for me, you and Gabriel would be walking off into the sunset together.'

'I don't think Gabriel's the walking-off-into-the-sunset type,' Maddie said, striving to sound light, flippant, but Susie didn't buy it.

'For you he could be,' she said, her face unhappy. 'For you he wants to be, and Charlie's right. This is all my fault. I know I shouldn't have been so rude to him but I was scared he might turn out to be like Andrew. That you'd fall in love with him, and then he'd leave you like Andrew did, so I thought…I thought if I was really horrible to him he'd either stick it out if he was one of the good guys or he'd go away quicker if he wasn't.'

'Oh, sweetheart, why didn't you tell me that's why you behaved as you did?' Maddie said through a throat suddenly so tight it hurt. 'If you'd only told me…'

'I've messed everything up, haven't I?' Susie murmured, and Maddie walked over to her and gave her a hug.

'No, you haven't,' she said firmly. 'Gabriel doesn't want to date me any more because he doesn't want to get involved with somebody with children. Maybe he might have hung around a little bit longer if you hadn't been rude to him, but he was always going to walk.'

'But if he doesn't want to get involved with somebody who has kids, why did he date you in the first place?' Susie protested.

Good question. 'I don't think he realised what he was letting himself in for,' Maddie replied. 'Now that he knows, he's decided he wants children, but he wants children of his own.'

'I suppose you can see his point,' Susie said. 'There can't be many men who would want to saddle themselves with an eight-year-old and a fourteen-year-old. OK, so I'll be off your hands in three or four years—'

'Susie, you will never be off my hands,' Maddie insisted. 'Even when you're forty-two, with children of your own, I'll always be there for you.'

Her niece's cheeks darkened. 'I know,' she said, her voice slightly thick, 'but, Aunt Maddie, we're not even your kids.'

'Sweetheart, I couldn't love you and Charlie more if I'd given birth to you,' Maddie said, willing her niece to believe her.

'But it's not right that you have to give up so much for us!' Susie exclaimed. 'You should have a life of your own.'

'I've *got* a life of my own,' Maddie protested. 'Susie, I have never considered you or Charlie a burden. There are times when you've driven me crazy, times when I could cheerfully have throttled the pair of you, but I will always love you, and when you're older—'

'You'll start living again?'

Maddie gazed at Susie, horror-stricken. 'I didn't say that—I have never for one second ever thought that. Susie, listen to me. I fell in love with Gabriel—there, I've admitted it—but you and your brother mean the world to me, and if Gabriel can't see that, if he can't understand I would never want to be without you, then he's not the man for me.'

'Honestly?' Susie said, and Maddie smiled.

'Honestly,' she said, and knew that she meant it.

Even if she could have waved a magic wand over Charlie and Susie to transform them into babies, she wouldn't have done it. They were Amy's children, her only link with a sister she'd loved dearly, and she wouldn't have wanted them to be anything but what they were.

'Gabriel doesn't know what he's missing, Susie,' she said. 'You and your brother are funny and smart, irritating and infuriating, wonderful and special, and if he can't see that then I feel very sorry for him.'

'I bet he doesn't feel sorry for himself,' Susie observed. 'I bet he thinks he's had a lucky escape.'

And Maddie managed a small, tight smile because she rather thought her niece was right.

'I just need you to countersign Ben Thompson's release papers, and he can be discharged today,' Jonah said as he and Gabriel walked down the corridor. 'His parents have asked if they can take his apnoea alarm home with him—just to give them a little extra security—and I've said they can have it for a month.'

'They do realise the alarm is only affixed to Ben's tummy by a sticker pad, and now he's a lot bigger he's quite liable to pull it off and give them a lot of unnecessary scares, thinking he's stopped breathing?' Gabriel said, and Jonah nodded.

'I've explained that to them, but you know what preemie parents are like. They may be desperate to take their babies home, but they also want a security blanket when they get them there.'

'How's Kieran getting on now?' Gabriel asked as he led the way into his consulting room. 'Any chest problems—signs of developmental delay?'

Jonah shook his head wryly. 'You're as bad as the parents, aren't you? He's fine. He's put on a pound in weight since he was discharged.'

'And Mr and Mrs Thompson are quite happy at the prospect of taking Ben home?' Gabriel said as he scrawled his signature across the discharge form and handed it back to Jonah. 'Some parents can panic at the thought of having to adjust to the presence of another baby when they've only just got into the routine of dealing with one.'

'They're over the moon,' Jonah said. 'In fact, according to them, no couple ever had such perfect babies, and you're the best doctor in the world.'

*Yeah, right,* Gabriel thought grimly. *Well, I'd prefer to be a less lousy human being.*

'Are you going back to the unit?' he said, and when Jonah nodded, he added, 'I think I'll come with you.'

Jonah looked startled. 'But you can't. You have Mr Phillips coming in to see you this morning. The representative of that charity group who seem keen to make a donation to the unit?' he added when Gabriel stared at him blankly.

'Oh. Right. I remember,' Gabriel said, though, in truth, he'd completely forgotten.

'No, you didn't remember, Gabriel,' Jonah said. 'Like you didn't remember your monthly Admin meeting yesterday, and we all ended up running around like headless chickens, looking for you.'

'Are you suggesting I'm losing the plot?' Gabriel snapped, and Jonah stared at him thoughtfully for a moment, then pulled over a chair and sat down.

'I'm not suggesting anything,' he said, 'but you've been behaving like a man who's living on another planet all week, and if there's something wrong—something I can help with—for God's sake, tell me.'

'It's personal, Jonah.'

'Maddie again?' Jonah grinned, then quickly smoothed out his features when Gabriel gave him a hard stare. 'Sorry. Look, I know these family dates are a pain, but—'

'It's got nothing to do with the family dates because we're not dating any more.'

Jonah's mouth fell open. 'You're not… But *why?*'

'It's not working out,' Gabriel said.

For a moment Jonah said nothing, then he cleared his throat. 'And who decided it wasn't working out—you or Maddie?'

'I did,' Gabriel said, and Jonah's mouth fell open even further.

'But, Gabriel, she's perfect for you. She's warm and kind,

and funny and smart… Look, whatever you've done—however you've screwed this up—get her back.'

'I don't want her back,' Gabriel flared, and Jonah stared at him in confusion, then suddenly his eyes narrowed and he looked grimmer than Gabriel had ever seen him.

'The reason you're not dating Maddie any more,' he said slowly. 'It wouldn't have anything to do with your realisation that there's no way on God's earth she'll ever apply for Lynne's job, would it?'

It was Gabriel's turn to look bewildered. 'What on earth are you talking about?'

'When you hired Maddie you said you were going to try to keep her sweet for four months in the hope that she'd step into Lynne's shoes,' Jonah said, his voice ice-cold. 'If these dates have been part of your keep-her-sweet plan, and now you've dumped her because you've realised your plan isn't going to work, you can have my resignation right now.'

'Of course I haven't been dating her because of Lynne's job,' Gabriel snapped. 'What kind of man do you take me for?'

Jonah met his eyes, glare for glare. 'You tell me.'

'I haven't thought about that for weeks,' Gabriel protested, and he hadn't. Not since the day Maddie had sat down opposite him in the canteen, looking panic-stricken and so very adorable. 'In fact, I don't know why I ever thought she would want to return to nursing in the first place.'

Because he was arrogant, he thought grimly, and arrogance always came before a fall. No, that's pride, but in his case arrogance and pride were pretty much the same thing.

'Gabriel, whatever the problem is, work it out,' Jonah said. 'If you let Maddie go—'

'You said you thought Nell might make a good ward manager,' Gabriel interrupted. 'If you still believe that, would you sound her out for me, see if she's interested?'

'Yes, but about Maddie—'

'I need to know if Nell is interested,' Gabriel said determinedly, 'because if she's not, we'll have to start advertising.'

'Yes, but Maddie—'

'I have nothing more to say about Maddie,' Gabriel said in a voice that brooked no argument. 'It's over. Finished.'

And it *was* over, he thought as Jonah left. His traitorous body might wish it wasn't but his mind told him it was better this way. He couldn't be a surrogate father to Charlie and Susie. If he was honest with himself, he'd never considered being one. All he'd wanted had been to make love to Maddie but, as he'd sat on the sofa on Saturday night and seen the photographs of Charlie and Susie smiling down at him, he'd known that he couldn't make love to her on the basis of a lie.

A woman like Maddie needed—deserved—more than a casual fling, and if he'd felt something tear inside him when she'd gazed at him, her eyes huge and bewildered in a face he knew almost as well as his own, then it was better this way.

*Or it would be,* he thought with a groan as he felt his body stirring and reacting to the memory of how she'd looked that night, her cheeks flushed, her lips parted, her breasts…

*Work,* he told himself, getting to his feet with a muttered oath. Stop remembering, and think about work. Think about next Wednesday.

Next Wednesday when he was going to meet Professor Larson of the Swedish Institute in Stockholm. Professor Larson, who never met individuals privately and yet who had, unbelievably, telephoned him on Monday to say he'd be in Glasgow in ten days' time and would like to meet him.

*Think about that,* he told himself. *Think about how it's always been your dream to work for the man, and if that doesn't stop you thinking about Maddie, nothing will.* Quickly he leafed through his appointment book to see what time he'd agreed to meet the professor, only to stare at the page in horror. There were six appointments listed, but none of them were with Professor Larson, and with a groan he grabbed his appointment book and hurried out of his consulting room.

'But, Maddie, I've agreed to meet Professor Larson a week today at two o'clock,' Gabriel exclaimed, dismay plain upon his face. 'I can't ring him up and cancel.'

'I don't see what else you can do,' she replied. 'If only you'd told me—'

'I thought I had,' he protested. 'I was sure I left a sticky note on your desk after he phoned on Monday but maybe my mind…' A slight tinge of colour darkened his cheeks. 'Maybe it was on other things.'

*Like how you walked out on me on Saturday night,* she thought, but she didn't say it.

'Can't you cancel some of my appointments?' he continued, and Maddie logged onto her copy of his appointment book on her computer.

'You have six meetings scheduled for next Wednesday. One is with the unit's biggest charitable benefactor, one is with the head of the health board and the other four are with individuals who I think we can also safely categorise as pretty important VIPs. Which ones would you suggest I cancel?'

'How about if you moved Mr Wilson's appointment from two o'clock to four o'clock,' he said desperately, 'and then moved Mrs Jeffrey's appointment from four o'clock to eleven o'clock in the morning—?'

'Gabriel, Mr Wilson made that appointment six weeks ago. Mrs Jeffrey made hers three months ago. OK, OK,' she continued as he groaned again. 'I'll see what I can do, but I can't promise anything.'

'Maddie, if you can pull this off, you can have anything you want,' he said fervently, and her heart twisted inside her.

*I want you,* she thought. Despite everything, she still wanted him.

*You're pathetic, Maddie,* her heart whispered. *This man has hurt you, dumped you, and yet not only do you still want him but you're trying to pull his butt out of the fire. He's screwed up, just like Colin and Andrew used to do, and just as you did with Colin and Andrew, you're trying to rescue him. You have learned nothing.*

'I'd get on with this a lot faster if you stopped hovering over me,' she said, injecting as much coolness into her voice as she could.

'Sorry,' he said, moving back a step, but it didn't help.

She could still smell his aftershave, was still intensely, acutely aware of him, of his nearness, of his breathing. Of him.

'Look, why don't you go back to your consulting room?' she said. 'If I find a way of changing your schedule, I'll let you know.'

He looked disappointed. 'I thought maybe I could help,' he said.

*Going away would help,* she thought. *Not standing anywhere near me would help, because when you stand close to me, I remember. I remember the touch of your hands on my body, the feel of your lips on mine, and I don't want to remember.*

'There really isn't anything you can do to help,' she said, all calm, cool efficiency on the outside, while inside her heart was beating so fast it would have brought the crash team to her side if she'd been attached to a monitor.

'You're sure?' he said.

'Positive,' she replied firmly, and after a moment's hesitation he nodded, but as he walked out of her office she bit her lip savagely.

How had she let this happen? She had been so sure she could safeguard her heart by making their dates family-only ones. She had been so certain that if she never spent time alone with him she would be safe, but somehow he'd got past her defences. Somehow, despite all the precautions she'd taken, she'd fallen in love with him, and now… What was she going to do? What the hell was she going to do?

'Are you OK?'

She looked up to see Jonah standing in her doorway and managed a smile.

'Fine, thanks,' she said. Apart from wanting to burst into tears.

'You're sure?' Jonah, said, scanning her face anxiously. 'It's just I saw Gabriel coming out of your office and—'

'He forgot to tell me he'd arranged a meeting with Professor Larson for next Wednesday afternoon and at the moment his schedule's so packed there's no way he can fit it in.'

'Professor Larson?' Jonah repeated. '*The* Professor Larson of the Swedish Institute in Stockholm?'

'The very same.' Maddie nodded, and Jonah let out a low whistle.

'I'm impressed.'

'Professor Larson isn't going to be if Gabriel has to cancel,' Maddie said dryly, and Jonah came round her desk to peer at her computer screen.

'You've not a hope in hell of altering that, Maddie.'

She didn't think she had either, but she was going to give it her best shot. Or at least she would try to give it her best shot, she thought with irritation as Jonah sat down on the edge of her desk, looking as though he was settled there for the duration.

'Don't you have people to see, places to go, Jonah?' she said.

'I've a ward round in ten minutes but… Gabriel told me you and he aren't dating any more.'

She stiffened in her seat. 'He told you that?'

'Not willingly, and he didn't tell me why.'

'I'm not telling you either,' she said, reaching for Gabriel's appointment book, only to see Jonah whisk it out of reach. '*Hey.*'

'I just want to say one thing, Maddie, and then I'll get out of your hair,' the specialist registrar said. 'The son of a bitch needs his head examined.'

She blinked. 'I…Thank you. I think.'

'Actually, I'd like to say one other thing,' he continued. 'It's not over until the fat lady sings.'

She waited for a second, then stared up at him uncertainly. 'Um, is that it?'

He grinned as he slid off her desk. 'For now, except… Are you really OK?'

'Of course I am,' she said, but she wasn't, and she knew Jonah knew she wasn't.

*Work, Maddie,* she told herself, reaching for her phone as Jonah left. *Figure out first how you can rearrange Gabriel's appointments so he can meet this Professor Larson next Wednesday, and then think about what you're going to do about the man himself.*

'Maddie, you are a genius, and whatever the hospital is paying you it's not enough,' Gabriel exclaimed with relief as he glanced down at his appointment book and saw the magical words, 'Professor Larson, 2 p.m.,' written in bold letters under next Wednesday's date. 'Mr Wilson, Mrs Jeffrey—all the other people I was supposed to see—they were OK about the changes?'

'They are now,' she said, remembering the initial ear-blasting she'd received from Mr Wilson, and the distinctly less than flattering assessment of her capabilities as a secretary she'd received from Mr Phillips. 'And you owe Jonah big time because he's giving up his day off next Wednesday to cover your ward rounds.'

A glimmer of amusement appeared in his dark grey eyes. 'Does he know that yet?'

'No,' she admitted, and he laughed.

A laugh that was deep and warm, and seemed to curl right round her heart, comforting it. Stupidly her heart lifted as his eyes met hers for a long moment. Then he looked away, shook his head and said, 'Thanks again for sorting out next Wednesday for me.'

'Not a problem,' she said, all sunshine bright, but it was, she realised, as she walked back down the corridor to her office, and there was only one solution.

She had to get another job. OK, so other people didn't resign when their office romances went sour but, then, other people's ex-boyfriends didn't promise they'd continue to come round to their homes to visit their nephews. Spending the next four months working with Gabriel, seeing him every day, making stilted conversation with him, avoiding eye contact with him, would be bad enough, but never knowing when he was going to turn up at her home? No, no way. She had to get another job.

'And next time make sure you get a good look at every member of staff before you sign on the dotted line,' she muttered. 'And if any of them are any younger than sixty, get out fast.'

'First signs, you know,' Lynne said as she passed her. 'Talking to yourself.'

'Oh, I'm way beyond the first signs, Lynne. I've moved into the certifiable stage,' Maddie said, and the ward manager laughed.

'Well, working for Gabriel does that to you. Did I ever tell you about the time—?' She frowned as her pager started to bleep. 'Oh, blast. No rest for the wicked.'

She was gone in a flurry of starched cotton, and Maddie walked into her office and stared with absolutely no enthusiasm at all at her overflowing in-tray. Sometimes she wondered if she was cut out to be a secretary. Maybe she should have retrained to be a teacher, except she couldn't have survived for three years without an income and the thought of trying to control thirty-five Susies was enough to make her blood run cold.

'You should have a life of your own,' Susie had said, and Maddie sighed.

She knew she should. She knew she shouldn't build her entire life around Charlie and Susie, that they'd ultimately grow up and want their independence, but it was too soon for her to return to nursing, no matter how much she might miss it. She'd stick with secretarial work for another two years, until she was sure Charlie was really settled, and then she'd return to nursing, but not at the Belfield. Never at the Belfield.

*And what about the personal side of your life?* her heart whispered, and she shook her head. She'd vowed once before that she was off men for the duration, but this time she meant it.

'Maddie, Gabriel wants you to phone the Scotts and get them in here as fast as you can,' Lynne said urgently as she flew into Maddie's office, looking tense and harassed. 'Tell them he's concerned about Diana's condition, but don't tell them anything else. Just get them in here.'

'But…' Maddie was talking to thin air. The ward manager had already gone, and Maddie's heart sank as she saw Jonah running down the corridor, closely followed by Gabriel, his white coat flapping.

Diana had been doing so well, overcoming all the infections she'd caught, but if she was being asked to telephone the little girl's parents, whatever had happened was serious, very serious.

Quickly she phoned the Scotts, and for once she was grateful that she knew nothing. No, she couldn't tell a panic-stricken Rhona anything other than Mr Dalgleish was concerned about Diana and, no, she didn't know any more than that, she told Simon, but could they, please, come in as quickly as they could.

'What's going on, Nell?' she demanded, hurrying out into the corridor as she saw her cousin pass. 'What's happened to Diana?'

'She seemed very lethargic when I came on duty this morning,' Nell replied, 'and then suddenly she started fitting. Jonah ordered an ultrasound and she's had a cerebral haemorrhage.'

'How bad?'

'Grade 4.'

Maddie's heart sank. A grade 4 was the worst there could be. Babies could survive a grade 1 or 2 cerebral haemorrhage, but a grade 3 or 4 would leave them severely brain damaged if not dead.

'Are Simon and Rhona on their way?' Nell asked, and Maddie nodded.

'They should be here soon.'

And they were. A little over half an hour later Rhona arrived, clutching her husband's hand, her face distraught, and as the couple disappeared into Gabriel's room Maddie's intercom beeped, and she hit the answer button quickly.

'Miss Bryce, could you come along to the consulting room right away, please?' Gabriel said, and Maddie's heart sank even further.

He was using his official I-have-somebody-with-me voice but she could hear the tension in it and reluctantly she got to her feet. Instinct told her she wasn't going to like this, and the minute she saw Simon's chalk-white face and Rhona's swollen eyes she knew her instincts were correct.

'This brain haemorrhage Diana's had,' Simon said as Maddie slipped quietly into a seat. 'I know it can lead to cerebral palsy, but cerebral palsy's not so bad, is it? A friend of mine's son has cerebral palsy and he's a lovely little lad. He has to use a wheelchair but his mental capacities are all there, and you can buy wonderful wheelchairs nowadays, real state-of-the-art things—'

'Simon, it's not as simple as that.' Gabriel interrupted gently. 'Diana's had a grade 4 haemorrhage, the most severe there is, and when a baby as vulnerable and premature as she is has a large haemorrhage, a lot of blood that should be in the bloodstream becomes diverted to the brain.'

'Mr Dalgleish, you didn't hear what my husband said,' Rhona protested. 'We don't care if Diana's disabled. She's our daughter, and we'll love her just the same.'

'Rhona…' Gabriel leant forward in his seat, his face almost as white as Simon Scott's was, his eyes dark with regret. 'Diana's circulation is collapsing. Her heart can no longer deliver blood and nutrients to her vital organs. Her kidneys aren't working any more, her liver has collapsed—'

'But people have liver transplants, kidney transplants,' Rhona interrupted desperately, 'and Maddie said you're one of the best—if not the best neonatologist in the country. That's what you said, wasn't it?' she continued, turning to Maddie, her eyes pleading. 'You said Mr Dalgleish was the best, so if it's a question of an operation, a transplant—'

'Rhona, I'm afraid there's nothing I can do,' Gabriel said, before Maddie could reply. 'I wish there was, but there isn't.'

'How…?' Simon swallowed. 'How long before…?'

'A few hours,' Gabriel replied. 'Probably less.'

A sob broke from Rhona. 'But miracles can happen, can't they? People who have been in comas for years suddenly wake up. People who are in awful, appalling accidents get better against all the odds, so maybe…maybe she can pull through this.'

Simon reached out and clasped his wife's hand in his. 'Rhona…Mr Dalgleish is saying there isn't any hope any more.'

Rhona looked across at Maddie, pain and grief and heartache etched on her face.

'There really isn't any hope?' she whispered, and Maddie shook her head.

'I'm sorry, Rhona—so very sorry,' she said, and Rhona drew in a shuddering breath.

'Can…can we see her?'

Gabriel got stiffly to his feet. 'We've moved Diana into a separate ward so you can stay with her if you want, until…'

'We'd like that,' Simon said with difficulty, then turned to Maddie. 'Would…would you come with us, too?'

'Of course I will,' Maddie said, and silently she followed the Scotts and Gabriel into one of the isolation wards they normally reserved for babies suffering from undiagnosed infections.

'She's so small,' Rhona said as she gazed down at her daughter. 'She's still so very, very small. Why couldn't it have been me? Why does she have to die when she's hardly lived at all?'

Maddie looked across at Gabriel in mute appeal, knowing there was no answer to this, there never was.

'Do you want to hold her, Rhona?' Gabriel said, and when Rhona nodded he carefully lifted Diana out of her incubator.

'I was going to show her the world, you know,' Rhona said, her voice breaking as she took Diana from him. 'I had all these plans, all these dreams. I was going to show her all the beautiful, magical things in the world, and now she's never going to see them, is she?'

Gabriel shook his head. 'No, she's not,' he said, his voice rough.

Gently Rhona stroked her daughter's cheek, then bent her head and kissed her. 'Diana, I will always love you. You won't be here with me, I won't be able to hold you, but I will always love you. You're my baby, my daughter, and you always will be.'

Tears were trickling down Rhona's cheeks, and Maddie could feel tears welling in her own eyes as Simon bent his head to kiss his daughter, too.

'Stay with us, sweetheart,' he said, his voice tight, restricted. 'Don't leave us. You're the most precious gift we've ever been given so, please...fight a little bit more. Fight to stay here with us, because without you...'

His voice broke, and Maddie had to look away because she had seen what the Scotts hadn't. Diana's frail chest was no longer moving up and down. She'd died while her father had been speaking, and she knew that Gabriel had seen it, too.

'Simon...Rhona...' he said softly, and Rhona looked up at him, saw what had happened in his eyes, and broke down completely.

Quickly Gabriel put his arm around her, then his eyes met Maddie's and she knew what he wanted. Though the Scotts had never seemed a particularly religious couple, they might welcome the help of the hospital chaplain. With a nod she slipped blindly out of the isolation ward, the sounds of Rhona's racking sobs tearing at her heart.

The rest of the day seemed interminable. Nobody talked about what had happened, everyone averted their gaze from the isolation ward, and never had Maddie been so glad when the clock on her office wall finally reached five o'clock.

To her surprise Gabriel seemed anxious to leave the hospital, too, and to her even greater surprise he seemed to have been waiting by the lifts for her.

'Rough day,' he murmured as they both stepped in.

'How are the Scotts?' she asked, and his jaw clenched slightly.

'Not good.'

She nodded. There wasn't anything she could say.

'I was wondering if I could come round this evening?' he said. 'See Charlie.'

'I'd rather you didn't, if you don't mind,' she said. 'Like you said, it's been a rough day.'

He looked awkward, uncomfortable. 'Actually, it's not so much Charlie I wanted to see, it's more...I've had a really lousy day, Maddie, and I could do with some company.'

She turned to face him, unable to believe her ears. Just who the hell did he think he was? He'd walked out on her on Saturday night and now he expected her to welcome him into her home and dispense tea and sympathy? OK, so he'd had a lousy day, but she'd had a lousy week and as far as she could see the weeks ahead weren't going to get any better, and they certainly wouldn't improve if she allowed herself to become his personal doormat.

'I'm afraid I'm busy tonight,' she said tightly.

'I wouldn't stay long—just an hour or so,' he said as the lift came to a halt on the ground floor and she stepped out. 'Maddie—'

'I'm busy, Gabriel,' she said, and turned on her heel and walked away.

## CHAPTER TEN

'NELL, being ward manager isn't really all that different from being a ward sister,' Lynne observed as she, Nell and Jonah sat in her small office drinking their morning coffee. 'OK, so there's a lot more paperwork—too much if I'm honest—but it's not as though you're new to the department. You know the staff, and the routine, and you've got seven weeks to pick my brains before I leave for New Zealand. You'll manage fine.'

'I hope so,' Nell said ruefully. 'Now that I've accepted the job, I don't want to let Gabriel down.'

'You won't,' Jonah insisted. 'And Gabriel isn't going to expect you to get everything right—not in the first few weeks.'

Nell nodded, but Lynne frowned slightly as she carried her mug over to the sink.

'You know, if you'd said that a month ago, Jonah, I'd have laughed in your face, but now… I just can't figure Gabriel out. For three years he was a complete pain in the butt to work for, then last month he became Mr Sunshine, and now suddenly it's like…' She shook her head. 'It's almost as though he's had all the stuffing knocked out of him.'

Nell shot Jonah a quick glance, and he gave her an I-haven't-said-a-word look back.

'He's probably just a little down because of Diana's death last week,' Nell said awkwardly. 'You know how he hates to lose a baby, especially one like Diana, who'd started to look as though she'd turned the corner.'

'Yes, but normally if we've lost a baby it's keep your head down, and don't say a word unless you want your butt nailed to the wall,' Lynne protested, 'but this time—nothing. Does Maddie know what's wrong with him, Nell?'

Nell looked like a deer caught in the headlights of a car, and Jonah came to her rescue.

'Shouldn't you be taking the files for our new intake of babies along to Gabriel, Nell?' he said, and she got quickly to her feet.

'And I suppose I'd better get back to work,' Lynne said reluctantly, but when the ward manager had gone Nell sat down again, her face troubled.

'What are we going to do about Maddie and Gabriel, Jonah? I've tried talking to her, but she keeps saying it's over, finished, and yet I know she's breaking her heart.'

'Gabriel says it's over, finished, too,' Jonah said ruefully, 'and if I try to talk to him about it, he chews my head off. I could shake the pair of them, I really could.'

'You know what's going to happen, don't you?' Nell said. 'Professor Larson will probably offer him a job this afternoon and Gabriel will head off to Stockholm, leaving Maddie in Glasgow, downright miserable.'

'Not if we can prevent it, she won't,' Jonah said.

'But, Jonah, there's nothing else we can do,' Nell protested. 'You've tried to speak to Gabriel, and I've tried to talk to Maddie, and we've got nowhere.'

'Which is why I think you'll have to talk to Gabriel, and I'll have to talk to Maddie.'

Nell's jaw dropped. 'I can't talk to Gabriel about something like this, Jonah. I hardly know the man, and it's so personal, so…so intimate.'

'Nell, you've seen the way Maddie looks at him when she

thinks no one's watching—the way he looks at her,' Jonah said. 'They're in love, and if we don't do something they're going to walk right out of each other's lives.'

'Yes, but…' Nell gulped. 'You know what Gabriel's like when he's in a temper.'

'He'd never hit a woman,' Jonah said firmly. 'He'd most certainly punch me if I tried to talk about Maddie again, but he'd never hit a woman.'

'That's good to know,' Nell said weakly.

'So, you'll talk to him?'

Nell chewed on her lip for a second. 'OK, I'll talk to him.'

But as she picked up the files and squared her shoulders, Nell wondered what the world record was for somebody getting a job and then losing it again, because she had a feeling she was about to break it.

'OK, let's recap,' Gabriel said, gathering up the files on his desk as Nell opened her notebook. 'I want ultrasound scans for Baby MacDonald and Baby Marshall. Baby Simpson is showing signs of jaundice, so she'll need phototherapy, and I want the ophthalmologist to check all of our new intakes' eyes, and the audiology technician to check their hearing.'

Nell's pen flew across her notebook for a few seconds, then she glanced up. 'Lynne thinks Baby Marshall's tummy is a little tense. It could just be after-birth stress, but…'

Quickly Gabriel extracted Baby Marshall's file from the pile in front of him, and flicked it open.

'Weight 1,500 grams,' he murmured. 'It could simply be after-birth stress, but it could also be necrotising enterocolitis—damage to his intestines due to an infection or poor blood flow. Set him up for an X-ray and let me know when the technician arrives.'

'Will do,' Nell said.

'Oh, and could you re-emphasise to Mr and Mrs Marshall

that touching can be extremely stressful for some very premature infants,' Gabriel continued. 'I explained that to them this morning, but they looked so shell-shocked by the sudden arrival of their son that I don't think they took it in.'

Nell nodded. 'I'll repeat the warning.'

'The trouble is it's an instinctive reaction to want to touch your child,' Gabriel observed, 'but parents forget that a baby has next to no tactile stimulation in the womb so if we can make sure that the Marshalls limit themselves to talking to their son for the next few days, that would be best.'

'I'll do that,' Nell said, and as she continued to make notes Gabriel sat back wearily in his seat.

Lord, but he was so tired. He couldn't remember when he'd last felt so tired, and he couldn't blame the weather. The hot spell had ended at the weekend with spectacular thunderstorms and torrential rain, bringing much cooler, fresher weather, but still he couldn't sleep. Night after night he tossed and turned, and always his mind kept returning to Maddie despite the fact that he knew he'd done the right thing—the only thing—he could have done.

Let it go, Gabriel, he told himself. It's the best thing for her, you know it is, so let it go, move on.

'You must be getting really excited about this afternoon,' Nell said as she closed her notebook. 'To meet a living legend like Professor Larson in the flesh… It's a real honour, isn't it?'

He nodded, but in truth he didn't feel like a man who was about to be given one of the biggest accolades of his medical career. Who would he share it with—who would really care? His staff were obviously thrilled to bits, and his parents would have been, too, if he'd still been on speaking terms with them, but there should have been someone special he could share it with, and there wasn't. Not now.

'Gabriel…'

He straightened in his seat guiltily. How long had he been

sitting there in silence? Now he came to look at Nell properly he could see she looked edgy and uncomfortable, and his heart sank. The only reason she could look edgy was if she'd changed her mind about the ward manager's job, and he didn't want her to change her mind. Jonah had been right. She was efficient, capable and completely on the ball, and if she didn't take the ward manager's job he'd have to advertise, and he didn't need that. Not right now.

'Nell, I know the ward manager's job must seem very daunting to you at the moment,' he said quickly, 'but Lynne is going to be here for another seven weeks, and I'm sure she'll go through everything with you—'

'I'm not worried about the ward manager's job—well, I am, but I'm sure I'll cope,' Nell interrupted, and to his surprise the colour on her cheeks darkened to crimson. 'It's… It's about Maddie. I know your relationship with her is none of my business—'

'Nell, I suggest you stop right there,' he interrupted, his voice positively glacial.

'Believe me, there is nothing I'd like better than not to continue with this conversation,' Nell said, her voice trembling slightly, 'but Maddie isn't just my cousin, she's my best friend, and she's miserable as hell, and I think you are, too.'

'She's miserable?' Gabriel said, wanting to believe her, realising to his dismay that he'd give anything to believe her.

'Of course she's miserable,' Nell said. 'She thought you were The One, and then you upped and told her you didn't want to see her any more. Wouldn't you be miserable if you were in her shoes?'

Gabriel thrust his fingers through his hair impotently. 'Nell, it wasn't a question of not wanting to see her any more. I can't…I can't give her what she needs. I can't be a surrogate father to Charlie and Susie. I'll screw it up, scar them for life.'

'Do you love Maddie, Gabriel?'

He did. He didn't know how it had happened, when his longing for her had changed into him loving her, but it had, and his face tightened.

'Yes. Yes, I do.'

'Then everything else will work itself out,' Nell insisted.

Gabriel shook his head. 'Love conquers all? Only in books and in the movies, not in real life.'

'Is this because Charlie and Susie aren't Maddie's kids?' Nell demanded. 'Is that what you can't cope with?'

'No, of course it's not!' he exclaimed. 'If they'd been babies, I think I might have been able to cope, learned how to relate to them, but I don't know how to talk to kids of their age, how to be on their wavelength.'

'Gabriel, you're not auditioning here for the part of super-surrogate father,' Nell protested. 'All Charlie and Susie want is somebody who will love their aunt. Somebody to be there for her—and for them—if they need it.'

A reluctant smile curved his lips. 'You make it sound so simple.'

'It's not, I know it isn't,' she admitted. 'But if you love Maddie, you can work through this.'

'And if I fail?' he said. 'If Charlie and Susie come to hate me, think I've failed them?'

'Gabriel, if you keep thinking you'll fail, then you're setting yourself up to fail. You have to *believe,* Gabriel. You have to think that everything's possible instead of thinking...thinking...'

'That a cow is a ruminating quadruped.'

'A cow is a what?' Nell said in confusion, and he smiled, but it was a strained smile.

'It's a quotation from a book somebody once suggested I read. What it basically says is you mustn't let facts and logic rule your head and heart. You have to allow dreams, and fantasy, and hopes in there, too, or you're not really living.'

'Can't say I've read it myself, but the writer sounds like he knows what he's talking about,' Nell said.

'Yes, but—'

'Gabriel, a logical person would say that with your lack of experience in dealing with kids, you're going to screw this up big time, but a person with heart would say that sometimes you just have to fly blind. Sometimes you just have to throw all caution to the wind and go for it.'

'Maybe.'

'No, not *maybe,* Gabriel,' Nell said. '*Definitely.* You have the dreams, and the hopes, and the craziness inside you. You just need to let them out, set them free.'

*Was she right?* Gabriel wondered as Nell left. He wanted her to be right because he knew, despite all of his attempts to convince himself otherwise, that he wanted Maddie back, and it wasn't simply to make love to her. He missed her more than he would ever have thought possible. He missed seeing her smile, missed spending time with her, missed funny little things like watching her run her fingers through her hair or seeing her stick her tongue out at Susie.

'I love her,' he said out loud to the empty room. 'I love her so much. Why the hell didn't I realise that before? How the hell have I been so *stupid*?'

And he *had* been stupid, because now he knew that he was going to have a marathon task to get her to believe him.

'What I need is a plan,' he told the clock on his desk, but it simply ticked on regardless, and he smiled a little ruefully. 'Fresh out of plans, huh? Well, me, too.'

'We have the results of the ultrasound scans Gabriel ordered for Baby MacDonald and Baby Marshall,' Lynne said as she stood beside Jonah and Nell in IC. 'Both show no abnormalities at the moment, but we're monitoring the situation.'

'Good, good,' Jonah said. 'Do you have a copy of the results?' Lynne nodded and, as she hurried away, Jonah glanced quickly over his shoulder to make sure none of the nursing staff were within earshot, then muttered, 'How did it go with Gabriel?'

Nell made a face. 'His main fear is he'll let Charlie and Susie down, fail them in some way.'

'Typical Gabriel,' Jonah said. 'Always wants to be the best at everything. But he definitely wants Maddie back?'

'The man's head over heels in love with her.'

'So all we have to do is convince him that he doesn't have to be super-duper surrogate dad, and that being an OK-he's-not-too-bad dad would be good enough,' Jonah said, and Nell sighed.

'Jonah, we can't convince him of that. He has to realise it himself, and if Maddie's not talking to him…'

'She'll talk to him by the time I've finished speaking to her,' he said, and Nell gave him an amused stare.

'You reckon? Jonah, I know Maddie better than you do, and if she's decided—as she has—that Gabriel's a complete waste of space, you're not going to get her to change her mind.'

'Nonsense,' he said bracingly, and Nell shook her head as Lynne came hurrying back.

'I'll remind you of that later, Jonah.'

'Jonah, I do not want to discuss Gabriel with you now or at any time in the future,' Maddie said, her brown eyes furious as she banged a pile of files into her out-tray. 'So if that's all you want to talk to me about, I suggest you turn right around and head out the door.'

'Maddie, you're throwing away something special here—'

'I prefer to regard what I'm doing as moving on,' she interrupted. 'Gabriel and I had a nice time while it lasted, but now I'm looking to the future, working out what I should do next.'

'Even if that means leaving behind the man you love?'

'Jonah, it wasn't me who wanted out. It was Gabriel, and he got out. End of story.'

Jonah shook his head. 'You know, I used to think Gabriel was the most stubborn individual I'd ever met, but you take the prize. Maddie, do you love him—want him back?'

'No,' she snapped, and he smiled.

'Liar.'

'I am *not* lying,' she protested, and the smile on Jonah's face widened.

'Maddie, this is me you're talking to. Whatever you say will go no further, so tell me the truth. Do you love him?'

For a second she said nothing, then she sat down wearily behind her desk. 'Jonah, it doesn't matter how I feel. It's over—done with. He doesn't want me and, though I'm a patsy where men are concerned, even I know when to call it a day.'

'Maddie, I think he knows he's made a mistake.'

She wanted to believe him, she so wanted to believe him, but she couldn't allow herself to. She'd spent too many nights tossing and turning, berating herself for being so stupid, for putting her heart on the line yet again, to be prepared to allow herself even a glimmer of hope.

'Psychic now, are you?' she said, not bothering to hide her sarcasm.

'I think if you were to give him an opening—meet him halfway—you might be surprised at what you hear.'

Why couldn't people leave her alone? she wondered as she stared at Jonah's earnest, concerned face. She felt stupid enough as it was, without people trying to convince her that somehow she could have a fairy-tale ending. There was no fairy-tale ending, and there never would be, not for her.

'Jonah, this conversation is closed,' she said. 'This conversation is never under any circumstances to be resurrected. Understand?'

'But, Maddie—'

'No, Jonah,' she said fiercely, and for a moment he hesitated, then he nodded in defeat.

'OK,' he said as he left, 'but I think you're making a big mistake.'

*I've already made one,* she thought. *I already let down my defences once, and I'm not about to do it again.*

She had an interview for another job next week. It was in a GP's surgery and, no matter how boring the work was or how obnoxious the GP turned out to be, if she was offered the position she was going to take it. OK, so it was further away from home, and when she'd spoken on the phone to the other medical secretary employed at the surgery her heart had sunk, but it didn't matter how nit-picking her co-worker was, she had to get out of the Belfield.

'Maddie…'

Oh, hell's bells, but she might just as well put a sign on her door saying, 'Maddie Bryce: feel free to harass her', she thought as she looked up to see Gabriel hovering uncertainly in her doorway.

'I'd like to talk to you,' he continued as she deliberately switched on her printer and began printing out the letters she'd typed that morning.

'I'm afraid I'm pretty snowed under, as you can see,' she said shortly, and out of the corner of her eye she saw him bite his lip.

Lord, but he looked so tired. Tired and stressed and unhappy. But she seemed to have spent most of her adult lifetime propping up men who looked tired and stressed and unhappy, and this time she was going to be tough, strong.

'But it's lunchtime,' he said, glancing at his watch. 'You have to eat, so I was wondering if we could perhaps go down to the canteen, talk there?'

Damn, he was right. It *was* lunchtime, and desperately she tried to think of some reason why she couldn't join him, only to let out an inward sigh of relief when Lynne appeared.

'Gabriel, we've another preemie on its way down from

Maternity. Male child, weight two kilos, with breathing difficulties. Gabriel, did you hear what I said?' she continued curiously when he didn't move, didn't even indicate that he'd heard her.

'I'm coming,' he said heavily, 'and we'll talk later, Maddie, OK?'

*Not if I see you coming first,* she thought, picking up her handbag as soon as he'd gone. *If I see you coming first, you won't see me for dust.*

This had to be payback for something, Maddie decided as she sat in the canteen and Doris Turner beamed back at her from across the table. Whatever she'd done in a past life it must have been truly horrendous for the gods to have decided she'd have the only vacant seat in the canteen next to her, and for Doris to have seen it with her beady little eyes.

'It's been so long since I last saw you,' Doris said, smiling at her with the smile Maddie knew only too well.

'Pressure of work—you know how it is,' Maddie replied. 'How are things in Obs and Gynae?'

'Of course, you won't have heard,' Doris said, all chummily confidential. 'To be fair, I wouldn't have known either if I hadn't happened to be passing Mr Caldwell's office, and his door hadn't happened to be slightly ajar, when he was talking to his wife, Annie.'

When you had your ear at the keyhole, you mean, Maddie thought.

'If this is something private between Mr Caldwell and his wife, then I really don't think you should tell me,' she said firmly, but Doris wasn't so easily dissuaded.

'Annie's pregnant.'

'Really?' Maddie said, temporarily forgetting that she disliked Doris intensely. 'Oh, I'm so pleased. So very pleased for both of them.'

'I've hinted to Mr Caldwell that perhaps this time she should stop working rather than trying to continue on as she did the last time with such unfortunate results, and I think he agrees with me but…' Doris sighed. 'I'm afraid Annie can wrap him round her little finger when she wants to.'

'I'm sure Annie will do what's right for her and her baby, aren't you?' Maddie said as calmly as she could, and Doris smiled a smile that held no warmth at all.

'Did you know that Dr Brooke and his wife are going on holiday next week?' she said. 'They're a really lovely couple, though their marriage did get into the *teeniest* difficulty last year. We had a locum, you see, who was filling in for Dr Dunwoody, and Helen—Dr Brooke's wife… Well, I'm not saying she was unfaithful but…'

Maddie gritted her teeth. How much more of this was she going to have to listen to? Maybe she could make a run for the door but, knowing her luck, Doris would just come after her.

'Doris—'

'And, of course, you won't have heard the latest about Mr Summers in Men's Surgical,' Doris continued. 'Apparently, he—'

'I'm afraid I have to interrupt you, Miss Turner,' a familiar deep voice declared, and Maddie didn't know whether to cheer or groan as she looked round to see Gabriel standing behind her. 'But I need Miss Bryce back in NICU right away.'

There was a glimmer of a smile in his grey eyes and she knew he didn't really need her back in the unit. He was rescuing her just like he had before, and she didn't want to be rescued. Or rather she did, but not by him.

It's the devil or the deep blue sea, Maddie, she realised, and got to her feet.

'Sorry about this, Doris,' she said with what she hoped was her best conciliatory smile, and before Doris could reply she was heading for the corridor, all too aware that Gabriel was following her.

'I hope I did the right thing,' he murmured when he caught up with her. 'I thought you looked rather like a deer caught in the headlights of a car, but if I shouldn't have butted in…'

'I'm glad you did,' she said, knowing she had to say it, and he smiled, a warm, wide smile that made her traitorous heart do a quick two-step in her chest.

'My pleasure,' he replied, his smile widening, and she quickened her step.

The unit. She had to get back to the unit. In the unit there'd be Nell, and Lynne, and she had a mass of work to do. In the unit she'd be safe.

Thank God there was the usual seething mass of humanity waiting at the lifts. Normally she hated getting far too up close and personal with people she didn't know, but today… There was safety in numbers and she needed safety, but to her dismay the safety net didn't last long. When they reached the second floor there was a sudden and noisy mass exodus.

'They must be giving away free catheters in Men's Surgical,' Gabriel said as the doors closed and they were alone.

*Jokes?* He was making jokes? Well, of course he was. Jonah had told her just how important Professor Larson was, how a visit from him could only mean one thing. Gabriel would shortly be saying goodbye to Glasgow and hello to Stockholm, which was fine by her. The further he went away from her the better.

'I'm glad the hot weather has finally broken,' he continued. 'I don't think we Scots are designed for it.'

'No,' she said shortly, then added, 'You haven't pressed the fourth floor button.' To her surprise, he didn't make any attempt to do so.

'I was wondering whether I could come round and see Charlie this evening?' he said instead.

*Not on your life.* 'I'm afraid we're going out this evening,' she lied.

'What about Friday, then?' he said.

'We're going to the cinema,' she said. Well, we are now.

'Then how about Saturday?'

'I'm afraid—'

'You're going out then, too,' he finished for her. 'Maddie, you agreed I could see Charlie—'

'I've changed my mind,' she said, stretching past him to press the fourth floor button, and the lift began its slow, creaking progress upwards. 'I think a clean break is better.'

'I don't,' he said, and to her amazement he hit the stop button and the lift shuddered to a halt. 'I want to see Charlie, and I want to see you, talk to you.'

'You can talk to me at work,' she said. 'And you—in case you've forgotten—have a very important meeting with Professor Larson in approximately…' she looked down at her watch '…ten minutes.'

'Screw the meeting,' he said, and her jaw dropped.

'Screw the…? Gabriel, this is *the* Professor Larson. The world-famous Professor Larson who is coming to the Belfield Infirmary specifically to meet you, and who—in case you've forgotten—you had me jumping through hoops for last week to rearrange your appointments. You *cannot* be late.'

'I can do whatever I damn well want, and right now getting you to listen to me is more important than any meeting I might have.'

'There is nothing you can say that I would be interested in,' she said stiffly, stretching past him to hit the start button. 'You've already made your position clear. I know where you stand, what you think.'

'No, you don't, and we're going to stay here until you do,' he exclaimed, pressing the stop button again, and Maddie moved from angry into incensed.

'Will you *stop* doing that?' She pressed the start button, but nothing happened. She hit it again and all the elevator did was judder. 'Oh, wonderful,' she snapped. 'Just wonderful. Now we're stuck. If you'd just left the damn thing alone and not kept hitting it like some overgrown schoolboy…'

'You hit it as many times as I did,' he pointed out. 'If *you'd* just left it alone, and listened to me—'

'So, what do we do now?' she interrupted. 'Suffocate?'

'Hardly,' he said. 'There's an emergency phone.'

'Then I suggest you use it,' she retorted.

He opened the small box on the wall, took out the phone and after a few seconds' conversation with Maintenance put it back again.

'What did they say?' she asked.

'They'll get on to it as quickly as they can.'

'But that could mean anything from five minutes to five hours,' she protested. 'And why didn't you ask them to tell the unit where you are, so Professor Larson doesn't think you've stood him up?'

Quickly, he reached out and caught her hands in his. 'Maddie, don't you understand even yet that I don't give a damn about my meeting with Professor Larson? *You* are the only one I care about. I was a fool to walk out on you that Saturday night.'

She pulled her hands free, and threw him a scathing look. 'Decided you ought to have had the sex, and then walked, have you? Well, I'm sorry but I'm not on offer any more.'

'Will you *listen* to me?' he roared, and her chin came up.

'Shouting will get you nowhere,' she said, her voice ice-cold. 'I have nothing to say to you, Gabriel Dalgleish, and there is absolutely nothing you can say to me that I would ever want to hear.'

'How about I love you, and I want to marry you?'

Her mouth fell open. He was teasing her—he had to be teasing her and it was a cruel joke—but he didn't look as though he was teasing her. In fact, his eyes were fixed on hers, deep, and dark, and liquid, and suddenly there didn't seem to be enough air in the lift for her to breathe. Could they be running out of air already? Surely they couldn't be running out of air already, but she was definitely breathless.

'Maddie, did you hear what I said?' he said gently. 'I said I love you, and I want to marry you.'

He didn't mean it. He couldn't mean it. She didn't dare allow herself to believe that he meant it.

'Maybe…maybe you want me,' she said unevenly, 'but wanting and loving… It's not the same thing, Gabriel.'

'I know it isn't,' he said, 'because though I want you—and God knows I do—what I feel for you I've never felt for any other woman before.'

'Gabriel—'

'No, please, let me finish. Before I met you…' He raked his fingers through his hair, his face pale under the fluorescent lighting in the lift, a muscle in his jaw quivering slightly. 'Before I met you I was only living half a life, and you… You brought sunshine and laughter, and all the things I didn't think mattered into my life. Hell, I wasn't even aware of them, let alone that they *did* matter. Now that I know there's more—so much more—I don't want to go back to the empty, lonely place that I was in before. I *need* you, Maddie.'

She needed him, too, she knew she did, but she had to keep a grip on reality. One of them had to.

'You might say that now—believe that now,' she said, 'but can you honestly say you don't wish I didn't come with Charlie and Susie attached?'

'Maddie, there's no point in us dealing with imaginary situations,' he protested. 'We have to face the situation as it is.'

'But if you could have the perfect scenario, wouldn't it be

just me without Susie and Charlie?' she persisted, and he sighed.

'It would certainly make things easier—'

'Well, there you go.'

'But that doesn't mean I don't want to try my level best to be a father to Charlie and Susie, if they'll let me. I walked away that Saturday night because I was scared of failure. I thought I had to be the perfect father, and somebody has explained to me that I don't have to be. I can be a so-so father, and it's still OK.'

She said nothing. She didn't know what to say. Part of her—a very large part—wanted to believe him, but the other part...

'Gabriel, you said you wanted to be a father yourself one day. What if I can't have children? What if we marry, and I discover I can't have children?'

'What if the sky falls down tomorrow and the end of the world comes?' he said. 'I don't know what will happen in the future. All I know is I want you by my side. You're lodged in my heart—as necessary to me now as the air that I breathe, the food that I eat—and I want to marry you, to take care of you, and Charlie and Susie, and to keep you all safe.'

He meant it, she could see in his eyes that he meant it, and a sob broke from her. A sob that had all the love and longing in his eyes replaced by horror.

'Oh, Maddie, don't cry,' he begged. 'I thought—I hoped—you might feel the same as I do, but if you don't...'

'I do love you, Gabriel,' she whispered. 'I will always love you.'

And before she could move, before she could do anything, he had wrapped her in his arms and was kissing her, and this time it was even better than it had been before because neither of them was holding anything back, neither of them had any secrets from the other any more.

'Oh, Maddie, I love you,' he said as he drew back, breathing heavily. 'Did I tell you that?'

'Once or twice,' she said, as breathless as he was, and he kissed her again, and she fell into his heat, loving the feel of his hands on her again, loving everything about him, and knowing that at last—*at last*—she'd finally got it right.

'When are you going to marry me?' he demanded. 'Tomorrow? Saturday?'

She chuckled into his neck. 'You can't marry anyone as fast as that, Gabriel. No one can. You have to go to a registry office—'

'Church,' he interrupted. 'I want the full works. You in a white dress, me in a morning suit, Nell as matron of honour, Charlie as a page boy, and Susie in a bridesmaid's dress, even if she is throwing daggers at me.'

'She won't—she actually really likes you,' Maddie said, then clutched hold of him as her knees suddenly seemed to give way. 'Gabriel, are we moving?'

'I like where you live now,' he said, planting a row of kisses along her collar-bone and making her shiver. 'It's the kids' home. It's what they know, where they're comfortable.'

'No, I meant—'

The rest of what she'd been about to say was lost as he kissed her again, and she clung on to him, drowning in his love, wanting him closer, nearer, knowing that she had never ever felt so happy, and knowing, too, that this was only the beginning.

'How do you think Susie and Charlie would feel about your fiancé staying overnight some time in the near future?' he said raggedly. 'The very near future. In fact, tonight?'

'I think they'd be delighted,' she said huskily. 'I know I would be.'

'Tonight, then,' he said fervently. 'Lord, but I want you now.'

'I want you, too,' she said. 'Maybe we'll be stuck here al

night. Maybe Maintenance won't be able to rescue us until tomorrow and I can think of lots of things we can do to pass the time.'

'Me, too,' he said, kissing her neck and lightly biting the spot he had kissed. 'In fact—'

*'Ahem,'* a voice suddenly said, and Maddie froze.

There was more air in the lift. She knew there was, and that could only mean one thing. Slowly she glanced over her shoulder, hoping she was wrong, but she wasn't. The lift doors were open and, worst of all, not only had they reached the fourth floor, but standing outside in the corridor was an acutely embarrassed-looking Jonah with a tall, distinguished-looking man with steel grey hair beside him.

'Professor Larson,' Jonah said, his voice coming out slightly strangled. 'This…this is Gabriel Dalgleish, and our…our medical secretary, Madison Bryce. Gabriel, this is Professor Larson.'

Gabriel stuck out his hand, all too aware that his shirt was half-open, and so was Maddie's blouse.

'I'm afraid you've caught me at rather a bad time, Professor,' he said.

'So I see,' Professor Larson observed, then his eyes twinkled slightly. 'I hope you are not quite so familiar with all your medical secretaries, Mr Dalgleish.'

Gabriel grinned, and looked down at Maddie.

'Only with medical secretaries who are shortly to become my wife.'